APT. 5

IS

ALIVE

Also by Russell Atwood

EAST OF A

LOSERS LIVE LONGER

APARTMENT FIVE IS ALIVE

BY RUSSELL ATWOOD

CONTENTS

a-part (@ p"art), *adv.* **1.** into pieces or parts; to pieces: *to take a watch apart; falling apart from decay.* **2.** separately in place, time, motion, etc.: *Our birthdays are three days apart..* **3.** to or at one side, with respect to place, purpose, or function: *to keep apart from the group out of pride.* **4.** separately or individually in consideration: *each viewed apart from the other.* **5.** aside (used with a gerund or noun): *Joking apart, what do you think?* **6. apart from,** aside from; in addition to; besides: *Apart from other considerations, time is a factor.* **7. take apart, a.** to disassemble: *to take a clock apart.* **b.** to criticize; attack: *She was taken apart for her controversial stand.* **c.** to subject to intense examination: *He will take your feeble excuses apart.* --adj. **8.** having independent or unique qualities, features, or characteristics (usually used following the noun it modifies): *a class apart.*

a-part-ment (@ p"art'm@nt), *n.* **1.** a room or a combination of rooms, among similar sets in one building, designed for use as a dwelling. **2.** a building containing or made up of such rooms. **3.** any room in a house or other dwelling: *We heard cries from an apartment at the back of the house.*

--Syn. 1. APARTMENT, COMPARTMENT agree in demoting a space enclosed by partitions or walls. APARTMENT, however, emphasizes the idea of separateness or privacy: *one's own apartment.*

apt., *pl.* **apts.** apartment.

APARTMENT 5 IS ALIVE

PREFACE

When we see an apartment for the first time, we consider the walls, the floor, and the ceiling.

But seldom do we look hard at the corners, the niches, and the slants in which the apartment lies and tells nothing but the truth. Slanted corner niches especially where everything collects and is rarely swept, too hard to reach and bothersome considering no one will ever notice, no one will ever see, no one will ever care. This is where debris collects, particles, follicles, shards of shattered crystal Christmas tree icicles, layered, mingled, packed, a crumb from a Dom Perignon cork lies crotched beside a crusted booger flicked discreetly out of sight at the same affair, emulsified by shed lint and dust, they remain so companioned unto dust (but such arrangements are not uncommon).

Most of the dust is composed of dead skin and dandruff flakes. Apartments are coated in it, the floors varnished with the daily tread-upon decay of human beings. The truth is tucked, swept, and forgotten in its corners, lodged and hardened like brittle grandma-candy, possibly never to be found, let alone eaten, but there. Lying there.

APARTMENT 5 IS ALIVE

CHAPTER ONE:

THE AMPUTATED ROOM

The Apartment knew.

How it knew, how much it knew, how much it understood of what it knew will all be gotten to, but first it must be understood that the Apartment knew or else nothing wonderful will follow.

This is not a ghost story. As far as the Apartment knew, ghosts did not exist. It had never seen or felt any (and It was uniquely placed to have noticed if there were: It was always there, in effect It was "there" and there was nothing "there" but the Apartment itself). No (parenthetically or not) when the Apartment was empty, It was empty. The only things that inhabited It were living.

This is not a haunted house story, because, one-- as previously stated--the Apartment would've known if It was haunted, and two, It wasn't a house; It was an apartment.

But this is where we enter into a gray area. It wasn't always an apartment. It began as a room in a house lived in by a family. And--house or not, haunted or not--this *is* a haunted house story.

***

Built in 1922, 65 Saint Mark's Place was one of several four-story brick-faced, slant-roofed rowhouses constructed between First and Second Avenue that year in lower Manhattan. It can hardly be imagined how abundantly tree-lined the sidestreet was back then, more like a country lane.

The family that moved into it were a father and a mother, two young girls (a year apart), a son still an infant, a grandfather and a grandmother, and an unmarried sister who gave piano lessons.

The Apartment knew nothing back then, it wasn't even an apartment yet. It was a room. More, it was the favorite room. Its windows looked out over a coppice of newly planted elms that over the years would gradually grow higher in their reach for the sky. It caught both a slant of morning sun and a slant of golden sunset that crept across the cherry wood floorboards like fingers on piano keys. It was the room where the piano resided and where the unmarried sister's lessons took place three days a week. It was where the birthday parties took place, where the Christmas tree went up, where they bobbed for apples on Halloween.

It was a beloved room and whenever visitors entered they said things like, "What a lovely room! So sunny, so fresh, so alive!" (but later, when It was an apartment, prospective tenants entered and said, "Small, isn't it?").

For the first four decades of its existence, the room knew nothing but blissful ignorance, no sense of past or present. Knowing nothing else, it had nothing to know. Such is the vicissitude of happiness.

Change crept in.

The boy died in the war in 1944. The grandfather the same year (the boy had been his favorite, named after him). The two daughters married and moved away. After that there were fewer parties and celebrations. The mother and father died within a year of each other and their wakes were held in the room.

From 1954 to 1961, the only two people living in the house were the unmarried sister---still teaching piano lessons on Thursdays and Fridays--and the grandmother who kept hanging in there, drinking her home-made brew of elderberry wine.   When she finally packed it in, the house became too big for the unmarried sister (for years she and the grandmother had only used the bottom two floors).   The husband of one of her nieces was in real estate and he made her a great offer on the building and found her a small house in Willamansett near where her other niece lived, and she adored it.   The neighborhood had changed a great deal and she no longer felt safe living on the Lower East Side of Manhattan.   Her piano lessons had dropped off, but three of her students had become professional concert pianists, so she could retire in peace.

It was her niece's husband's idea to break-up the four-storey rowhouse into 12 individual apartment units, no idea this decision would bring about dozens of weird mutilations and deaths.

The building had to be gutted to some extent to accommodate more plumbing, additional wiring, and a shaftway constructed so each unit had a flow of air.

First of all, the room was cut in half.   A wall built bisecting it.   The room lost two of its windows. After that, the room remained more or less intact while the sounds and vibrations of destruction surrounded it.

The workers used the room to dump all their belongings and equipment they carried in in the morning, and during the day mixed their plasters and paints there as they went about renovating the rest of the building with new walls, new ceilings, new fixtures, adding a new gas range, toilet, and combination bathtub/shower to every unit.   In the end, the room was the last on the list to be renovated, but by then, money was running thin on the project, so only the most minimal amount of work was done on the room. Ceiling, walls, floor, marble mantle, chimney, fixtures, were left as they were. Plumbing was installed to make a small kitchen sink beside the door that lead to the outer hallway and stairs, where before two doors swung open to reveal the grandeur of the room, now just this single metal door with a peephole in it.

And what had once been a roomy cloakroom had been converted into a narrow bathroom with a toilet and combination bathtub/shower, but no sink.

Its original glass four-panel window frames were sledgehammered out. Two new energy-efficient metal windows were installed in their place like dentures. Its wooden shutters were left intact, but folded away and painted shut in their recesses. Similarly, the room's fireplace had its chimney sealed and a metal plate installed and painted over.

As for the rest of the room, they left it as it was: half of what it had been.

The Apartment didn't understand what had happened to It. It didn't "know" yet, but It was aware, aware of the change.

It seemed only a moment ago everything had been perfect. And now, somehow, the house was gone and It was alone. Apart, not a part of a whole, because there was no longer a whole except the hole all around It where Its house used to be. Taken apart, broken into pieces, carted away, replaced by new pieces. Everything, except for the room, halved and half-finished, half and half-not, and not a room anymore but an apartment. The Apartment felt this schism and awful vacancy. It knew nothing but loss, being a fragment of what It had been, the victim of an amputation in reverse: the body cut away, removed, and the single limb left behind to feel phantom pain.

In 1963, the first tenants moved into It.

CHAPTER TWO:

FAMILY OF FIVE

The Apartment had led a sheltered life as a room, a lot of the nasty things about living people had taken place in other rooms of the house (a wayward fart the worst it had to contend with for four decades). Now people were living in it and it was full of cooking, shitting, smoke, spitting, more cooking, more shitting, vomiting, pissing, more cooking, more shitting; this seemed to the Apartment the tenants' predominant occupation. It was used to piano recitals and teacakes, not goulash and gastritis.

And often the people were naked. The Apartment was used to having people with their clothes on in It. It liked clothes on people; it was like a coat of paint on your walls, not the ugly underneath. Possibly the Apartment was a prude, but It was all surface--walls, ceiling, floor--and could only judge by surfaces and It didn't like what was inside of It.

As a room, it had been the setting for merriment, celebration, the occasional secret kiss. All the negative emotions were displayed elsewhere, behind locked doors in other rooms. Now, as an apartment, all was clustered inside of It, the good and the bad.

The Apartment didn't care for people, didn't like what they did, how they smelled, what they spilled. They were ugly, at least their surface was, and the apartment only understood surface because it was all surface: a ceiling, walls, and a floor. These surfaces designated its parameters and it judged the people inside it at surface value. And the surface it witnessed was of people behind closed doors. Not their outdoors surface, their surface in mixed company, but their alone surface, their real surface, uncensored, unmasked, naked. All the Apartment knew of what lay below was in the variety of wetnesses they spilled on its surface. At best the Apartment tolerated their occupancy. It was indifferent to the violence and misery that dwelt within it. So It did not deliberately set out to kill the family inside of It.

***

It was the first time the Apartment made it into the newspapers. A family of five was living in It. A man, a woman, an older woman, and two children, little boys who slept in the same box bed in a corner of the Apartment.

The Apartment had nothing against the two little boys, they were quiet, mostly out of fear, and the games they played when the man was away never damaged the Apartment.

The woman and the older woman, likewise, the Apartment had nothing against, except maybe for the smell of the older woman's cooking which consisted largely of cabbage, but otherwise the Apartment tolerated the two women.

The man.

The man the Apartment could live without.

He was gross, he was fat, he was loud, he smoked cigars, he drank (and drank and drank), he stank, he spit on Its floors when it suited him, he spanked the boys with a leather strap, slapped the woman, and shouted and spit at the older woman.

All the Apartment could do was take it, endure it. It had no choice.

One night the man came home very drunk. Louder than usual, tripping up the stairs and swearing as he tottered from handrail to wall.

When he got to the door of the Apartment, the man already had his key out in front of him.   For two minutes he played pin-the-tail-on-the-donkey trying to get it into the lock, along the way scratching the paint off the surface of the door in striated lines.   On the ninth attempt, the key entered the lock and he turned.

Only it wouldn't turn.

He grunted.   He twisted and turned the key, only it didn't turn, it wouldn't turn.

Finally, he pounded on the door and bellowed, "Open up!"

The woman was out of bed in a shot.   She ran to the door and turned the knob.   It wouldn't turn.

The man pounded on the door.

"Open up, you bitch!"

"I'm trying."

"You better open this door."

"I'm trying."

"Lock me out of my own home!   I pay for this shithole.   Open up, you--"

"I'm trying, I'm trying, I'm trying!"

And soon the older woman was beside her and they both were trying.

The man raged on the other side of the door and the older woman pleaded, "Quiet, please, it is stuck.   Stuck."

The man went silent.

"What did you call me?" the man said, shocked by what he thought he heard the older woman say. "Open this DOOR!"

"Go back to bed," the woman told the two little boys.

In the hallway, the man went berserk.   He beat on the door with his fists, his elbows, his thighs, his knees, his hips, the heels of his feet, his head leaving dents in the metal surface of the Apartment's door and a lather of grease, spit, sweat, and snot.

At the height of this, the Apartment door swung open.

The man exploded in.

The little kitchen was to his left as he came in. So was the sink's draining board and upon it the large knife the older woman used to chop up her cabbages.

The following day's newspaper headline was: MAN KILLS FAMILY, SELF.

***

In March 1971, a fire broke out in one of the rear ground floor apartments.

The Apartment no longer had any connection with the rest of the building, but it felt some of the heat and the excitement. It preferred the acrid smoke over the human smells Its surfaces had accumulated. Part of it welcomed the spread of flames, wished to be engulfed. Burn wood burn, destroy the atrocity It had become. It enjoyed the thrill. The revolving red lights of the firetrucks shooting through the windows and playing over Its walls and ceiling. The firemen in their bulky uniforms, carrying hoses and axes, clomping around the stairwell in their boots, telling the tenants they had to evacuate. Telling them they had to leave, and they left. The Apartment liked all of that, but didn't know why. Why It was alone, why It was bitter, why It felt anything at all when It would rather feel nothing, be nothing.

But the fire was contained and put out.

***

The first time It killed a mouse came as a great surprise to the Apartment.

The mouse was in the walls, had tunneled its way from one apartment to another and finally come to apartment #5, at a time when It was vacant, between tenants.

The little gray mouse began nibbling and clawing at a crack in the wood on the other side of the Apartment's baseboard.

An annoyance to the Apartment that disturbed it from its unoccupied state.

The mouse was weak and hungry and had nothing better to do than persistently nibble and scratching and get on the Apartment's nerves.

Finally the mouse gnawed an aperture just large enough to poke its tiny head all the way through and look around.

The Apartment involuntarily closed the hole like a constricting sphincter and--snick--the mouse's severed head (no bigger than a gumball) dropped to the floor as neatly as a guest of Madam le Guillotine's. Welcome to Apartment #5, little mousey. You wanted in so bad. Enjoy your stay and decay.

No trace of the hole or the nibbling remained on either side of baseboard, just smooth over-painted wood just as before.

The Apartment hadn't known it could do that.

The Apartment didn't know how it could do that, the action was completely involuntary except for the emotion behind it.

Could It do it again?

***

The rest of the building's apartments acquired more long-term tenants who stayed on for years, but Apartment #5 had a big turnover rate . It was the least attractive apartment in the building, true, with its sloping floor that slanted southward and its half-finished look, but it was the pervasive air of dejection that turned people off and sent them elsewhere. No one stayed longer than a year in the Apartment. Some died within it.

Other tenants in the building whispered about the Apartment as they walked softly past Its door.

The Apartment registered the passage of time through the rhythm of the city, the vibrations that were sent up through the building's foundation and structure, the flow of delivery trucks and buses in the daytime, the soft suss of taxi-cabs and foot-traffic in the evening. And the people inside it operated on a rhythm, sleeping at night (most of them), rising to leave in the morning, returning at night to refill the designated space with odors and motion and sound. People were the Apartment's clock, their coming and going the ticks and tocks. When people weren't inside It, Its clock stopped. The Apartment welcomed this dormancy.

The neighborhood changed. In 1973, extra locks were installed on the Apartment's door and a gate attachment to the window to the fire escape.

Then, in 1977, a new tenant moved in. And everything changed.

CHAPTER THREE:

THE ODD COUPLE

The seed of the Haunted House parties was planted in the mind of Jerome Schwartz when he was eight years old reading one of his older brothers' pulp magazines, seeing the term "Grand Guignol: in a story by a man named Bloch.   Jerome promptly looked it up in his copy of Webster's Elementary Dictionary for Boys and Girls, but couldn't locate it.   This intrigued him, so he wrote it down and the next time he went to the public library, looked it up in the Adult Section's dictionary.

Grand Gui-gnol *(Fr. gRa"n   ge-nyo^l'),*   **1.** a short drama stressing horror and sensationalism.   **2.** noting, pertaining to, or resembling such a drama. [after *Le Grand Guignol,* small theater in Parish where such dramas were played].

It was only a paragraph entry, but it spoke volumes to young Jerome.   He knew everything about it in an instant, as if he had always known of it, just not what to call it.   And he knew it was what he wanted to do. No matter that it was a form of theater that had flourished in the 1800's and disappeared.   The distance of time meant nothing to him.   200 years ago was as far away as last summer to him at eight years old.

Beside the entry in the dictionary was a photo illustrating one of the scenes from a typical Grand Guignol: a woman in a white nightgown having her head sawed off by a man with a long black beard. They were both obviously heavily made-up actors, hamming it up, but the sawing off of the woman's head looked real. It made Jerome spontaneously laugh, because it was both "fakey" and real at the same time. The fact that horror made him giggle stuck with Jerome. Not real horror--he knew of real horror, knew from overheard conversations of his relatives what had happened to Jews like him in Nazi Germany. And he was a naturally compassionate child, cried if he saw others in pain (which made some of his family laugh, "What a schlep!"), took no delight in the suffering of others, and went out of his way to alleviate it whenever he could.

But fakey-horror he loved. Revered.

Jerome Schwartz lived in Brooklyn, the youngest of five children, two older brothers and two older sisters. He was the baby of the family, and as a result was coddled and indulged in his artistic endeavors.

He had beautiful green-blue eyes and curly black hair and a smile that melted people's hearts. He loved to color and draw and paint, and his family praised his every new finger-painting or clay sculpture. He danced and did impersonations of his relatives to the applause and delight of his entire family.

His first endeavor at an early age into what would later become known as his *illusions* was to draw a screaming face on a paperbag, fill it with some of his father's shaving cream and 3 drops of his mother's red confection food-coloring, shake it up--gently, artistically--then brought it outside to the sidewalk to show his waiting friends, his audience.

He put the bag on the ground, then raising his foot above it, he stomped down on the screaming face. The red-dyed shaving cream burst out all about their feet like a fireworks display. His friends all laughed and cheered, and even the girls screamed, "Do it again! Do it again!"

Not that all the girls liked Jerome's *illu*sions, but the weird ones did, and Jerome liked the weird ones.

Janice Weston, for one, who at 16 had a gray streak in her raven black hair that drove Jerome wild.

And Kimberly Fitchet, whose left eye was blue and her right eye was green-grey, and long blond silky hair spun gold. And boobs like...well, boobs. He had no real preference, he loved boobs in all shapes and sizes. Nipples like blue jeans' rivets or areolas like teacup saucers. And, as he discovered later in life, the weird ones put out, so Jerome had no problem with that.

The seed was planted. It flowered twelve years later when Jerome moved to Manhattan. Public acclaim set his path and it led him to 65 Saint Mark's Place, Apartment #5.

When he was eighteen he enrolled in New York University, in the heart of Greenwich Village, to study art. To meet his tuition, he worked part-time as a stockboy at Macy's department store. One early November day, he was sent to assist the store's window-dresser, Mr. I. V. Kent, in installing that year's Christmas window display. Some of the props were heavy and some weren't as heavy as they looked; when Jerome bent down to lift a realistic-looking fireplace, he nearly threw it over his shoulder, expecting the weight to be much greater. It made Mr. Kent laugh, it was a great compliment, and he took an instant liking to Jerome. And even after he learned Jerome liked girls--liked them a lot--they still got along, because Kent was an artist, too. He clued

Jerome into a secret that would change his life forever.

"Forget painting! Forget sculpting! What? You paint a picture, the best you ever could. So? Maybe you're lucky the best you can hope for it ends up hanging in the Metropolitan or the Louvre! You know how many paintings they got in the Louvre (Kent kept pronouncing it LUVE-rah)? Thousands upon thousands, and you? You're competing with Rembrandt and Van Gogh. So you? You are probably hanging outside the toilet or maybe *in* it. Hanging in the loo in the Louvre.

"Now look at me. My museum is a full block of Fifth Avenue mid-town Manhattan, the city that never sleeps. My displays are always on display!"

It wasn't a boast. It was the damn truth, and Jerome knew it.

"Sure," Kent said, "no one knows your name, but my real name is Irving Verites Kentopolous, so better they shouldn't know it."

Jerome waited for Kent beside the timeclock that evening after he clocked out. Kent raised his eyebrows, surprised, maybe his radar had been wrong. He regarded Jerome with a hungry smile, until the poor boy stammered out that he wanted to learn window-dressing.

Kent shrugged his shoulders, it took all kinds to make a world.

"Sure thing, kid. I'll show you the ropes. You seem to have a natural feel for it anyway. But Jerry boy, as sweet as I am on you, you ever deliberately underbid me for a job and I'll cut your nuts off with a linoleum razor."

The next day, Kent spoke to the store manager, explained his need for an assistant, and that afternoon Jerome was transferred to the window-display department (with no change in salary) and became Mr. Kent's apprentice.

Jerome dropped out of NYU. He began learning more from Kent than he ever had in a classroom. The most important trick--or law--of window-dressing Kent passed onto Jerome was: NGSI, Nobody's Gonna See It.

"All you got to worry about, kid, is what the eye takes in: The Front. Behind-the-scenes is just that. Sheesh! Worked with a guy once, we're putting in a Spring sale's display at Lord & Taylor's. I'm doing the flowers, he's making the trees. He's got this cardboard cut-out of a tree about six feet tall--looks great--but I see him and he's painting *both* sides of it. Why? I ask him. He tells me--like he's proud of it-- 'I'm a purist.' Purist-smurish. It took him twice as much time and twice as much paint. 'Go be a purist on your own dime,' I tell him. Never worked with that guy again.

"Once I put in this 'Ice Sculpture' here at Macy's. It was made entirely of packing crates I got from Fulton Fish Market, painted silver and wrapped in cellophane, but the store manager first time asks me, 'What happens when it melts?' Haha, people still remark on it, ask me if I'll ever do it again."

Within a year, Jerome was working full-time at Macy's and received enough of a pay-increase that he could move out of his family's home in Brooklyn and get his own apartment.

He saw an ad in the classified section of *The Village Voice* for a studio apartment in the East Village, and during his lunch hour ran downtown (literally "ran") to the offices of Roethke Realty. They gave him a key to the apartment so he could go check it out on his own. With only twenty minutes left on his lunchbreak, he ran there as well, and up the front stoop, and up the one flight of hallway stairs to the door of Apartment #5.

He burst into the apartment huffing and puffing, made one complete tour of it, then stopped breathing for a moment.

It was love at first sight.

He checked his watch. Still seventeen minutes before his lunchbreak was over. He hit the sidewalk running to his bank's closest branch. He withdrew enough cash to cover both first and last month's rent. Ran like a maniac back to Roethke Realty and told them, "I'll take it."

He was late getting back to work that day, but it was worth it: he had a signed two-year lease and keys to his very own apartment. He couldn't wait for the workday to end.

***

Before Jerome Schwartz moved into It, people had always just been obstructions lodged inside the Apartment, It welcomed new tenants as a body welcomes tumors, polyps, and cancerous lumps.

But from the very start, the new tenant was different, his rhythms ran contrary to the light and dark outside. When he returned at night, he didn't cook smelly food and then finally fall asleep. He worked through the rare quiet hours, in New York City between three and five A.M. He built a Model-T Ford, a Converse high-tops sneaker as big as a motorcycle, a smiling yellow Sun, a droopy-eyed Moon, and more. He never stopped. And none of it ever stayed. As soon as the paint and glue had dried, they left the Apartment and never came back.

The new tenant stunk like all people do, but never cooked in the Apartment, always ate take-out from a delicatessen. He drank whiskey but never spilled a drop of it on the floor. He stunk of perspiration from the work that he did, and the smell didn't bother the Apartment.

When he first moved in, instead of slapping a new coat of paint on the walls, the new tenant laboriously peeled away the layers of overpainting that concealed the original design of the corner moldings, the marble of the mantelpiece, and best of all, it freed the window shutters that had been painted shut for two decades when It first became an apartment. Brought back memories.

For Jerome, Apartment #5 was his workshop and always would be. He rarely slept there. He maintained a string of three women he booty-called daily on loose rotation, making his call whenever he'd wrapped up his work for the night, usually about two hours before dawn and three hours before any of the ladies had to go off to work, then he would spend the rest of the day sleeping at their place and eating out of their refrigerator.

In the Spring of 1978, he started his own freelance window-dressing business. At first his clients were smaller establishments, drugstores and appliance shops, but then he landed work with Waldenbooks in the Flatiron District. His first job for them, it was also almost his last.

The Haunted House parties started because Jerome did *too* good a job, went too far with the window displays he created for the bookstore in October 1978.

The bookstore's permanent window-dresser had become seriously ill and they needed a replacement for an important rush-job. A new definitive edition of *The Complete Works of Edgar Allan Poe* had been published by Scribner's and Waldenbooks was pushing it hard for Halloween. They needed someone who could design and build four full window displays by the weekend. Two other agencies had turned the job down as impossible to do in so short a time, but when they called Jerome, he told them, "Not a problem."

He worked like a demon, three days without sleep. He built everything in his apartment, mostly from midnight to dawn. Once one display was completed, he dismantled it, transferred it to the bookstore, and reassembled it in its window. Then returned to his apartment and he began the next.

He designed four displays depicting "The Tell-Tale Heart," "The Cask of Amontillado," "The Pit and the Pendulum," and "The Premature Burial."

Working only with heavy-duty corrugated cardboard, fishing line, nylon stockings, and paint, he created displays worthy of Madame Tussaud's Chamber of Horrors. But...only when viewed in a certain light--light and shadow were the secret ingredients--which was where the problem came in.

On Sunday morning--the day the bookstore was closed and only the cleaning crews inside--he removed the covering brown paper from the inside of the windows and unveiled the four completed displays. He went outside to view the result.

He felt sick to his stomach. It looked like a third-grader's art project, shabby and ridiculous. He had made it all with only cardboard, fishing line, nylons, and paint--and that's *exactly* what it looked. He was ruined. He must've been mad. What had he been thinking?

He walked away in a daze, dragging his feet all the way back to his apartment. Without bothering to lock the door behind him, he flopped down on a pile of cut-up cardboard, and fell into a troubled sleep of sheer exhaustion, his mind repeating over and over again, "I'm ruined."

When his telephone rang and woke him, he temporarily didn't know the day or the time. The apartment was dark and streetlights were on outside. He fumbled for the receiver.

"Yeah?"

"Jerry, you're a freakin' genius, man!"

"Wha? Who is this?"

"It's Don."

"Oh. What ya talkin' about?"

"Your windows, man."

My windows. Oh god. It all came back to him. He was ruined.

"I know," Jerome said, "I--"

"They're amazing!"

"Huh?"

It took his friend awhile to convince Jerry he wasn't razzing him, just yanking his chain because the windows looked so feeble and amateurish.

"No, man go look for yourself, you don't believe me. There's mobs of people in front. Like Macy's at Christmas."

Jerry caught a cab back to Waldenbooks, but had the driver let him out a block away.

People were standing out front, not mobs, but three or four at each window, but whenever someone passed their interest was sparked and they had to see why others had stopped and so they were stopping, too.

Jerome crossed the street and joined them and saw what they saw. There it was, his Grand Guignol, just as he'd conceived it but hadn't seen before.

The wild eye of Fortunato before the last brick is fitted into his tomb. The blade of the pendulum glistening with the gore of the Grand Inquisitor's victims. The tell-tale-heart exposed from torn-up floorboards seemed to throb with life. The transformation was shocking. But how?

The answer was obvious, he had created it in the dim lights of his apartment and it only came to life after-dark, when the shadows were starker, when the opposing beams of red and green lanterns crisscrossed and clashed sublimely.

His eyes welled with tears. It was beautiful. He wasn't ruined after all. He was a success. Waldenbooks would probably hire him full-time after this.

He dropped a dime at the nearest payphone and called up his friend Don and they went out to celebrate. He slept peacefully that night, in his own apartment for a change. Life was good.

Until the next morning at just past eight o'clock when the bookstore's manager, Mr. Morgenstern called him on the phone.

Jerome thought he was calling to compliment him on a job well done.

"Mr. Schwartz, come here now and remove this trash from our windows before we open at ten."

"Uh...do you mean--"

"Mr. Schwartz, this is not at ALL what we were led to believe of your work. We trusted the recommendations we received, but this--THIS--is unacceptable!"

"Mr. Morgenstern, I--"

"Before we open at ten o'clock," Mr. Morgenstern said.

"Yes, sir, I'm very sorry, Mr. Morgenstern. I--"

But Morgenstern had hung up.

Jerome was back on the sidewalk in front of his window displays by half-past eight, and he saw what

Mr. Morgenstern had seen when he came in that morning. The displays were again as shabby and childish as he'd seen the day before and no longer how they looked the night before.

How could he explain all this to Mr. Morgenstern? He couldn't. He accepted that. Better to grovel with his tail between his legs, apologize and promise to fix it. Which is what Jerome did.

Mr. Morgenstern liked Jerome Schwartz, it was his idea to hire him, which was why his disappointment was so great on Monday morning. But Jerome appeased him, explained that sometimes a concept doesn't come off, but he had another idea--a scarecrow motif (which Jerome initially discarded as too pedestrian), but Mr. Morgenstern agreed to give him a second chance if he could have it installed by Wednesday.

The Scarecrow window display--which Jerome threw together in two hours that afternoon--was a big success, with Mr. Morgenstern and the customers.

And the Edgar Allan Poe display was all transferred back to his apartment.

But it didn't end there. When his circle of friends discovered what had happened, they perceived it as censorship and Waldenbooks' name became a curse upon their lips. Incited by his friend, Don, a boycott was planned. After having mollified Mr. Morgenstern and securing further work, a boycott was the last thing Jerome wanted. So he acted quickly to quell the uprising and announced everyone could see the displays up-close--not under glass--in his apartment at his Halloween party on October 31st.

And that's how it started, the first of 17 legendary Haunted House Parties in Apartment #5, from 1978 to 1996.

Jerome boxed-up all his tools and supplies, and bagged his laundry and stuck them all in the closet on the highest shelf.   Then he re-assembled Poe's Tales of Terror window-display in the apartment.   But he couldn't resist tweaking things a bit.   Out of red ripe cherries he fashioned Fortunato's bulging eyes.   He coated the pendulum's blade with corn syrup and bedazzled it with sparkly g-strings, so they hung and dripped like gore.   And in recreating The Tell-Tale Heart, Jerome lifted one of the Apartment's floorboards--the key slat, shorter than the rest, that was fitted last into place and screwed down, not nailed, in case the floor ever need to be taken up again--and in the recess below nested a heart he made out of strawberry Jell-O spooned into a nylon stocking and tied together with fishing line, and all lit from below with a flashlight that flickered and gave the impression of throbbing.

As a final touch he called a Brooklyn ice distributor and ordered four blocks of dry ice.   He set one up in a tub in each corner of the room.   Once water was poured over them, a thick film of swirling fog blanketed the floor,   A fog machine would've been more economical, but Jerome had worked with them before and didn't like the smell produced by the propel mineral oil it burned.   Fine for theater, but bad for a party.

He worked until the last minute, dimming the lights just as the streetdoor buzzer rang and the first guests arrived for the first Haunted HouseParty at 7 P.M., Wednesday October 31, 1978.

He opened his door to a green-skinned, fiery-red-haired girl dressed in a silver lame' tubetop and mini-skirt escorted by the current President of the United States, Jimmy Carter.

The green-skinned woman aimed a plastic raygun at Jerome, when she pulled the trigger it spit out tiny sparks.

"Beep-beep, TAKE ME TO YOUR BOOZE, beep-beep."

"Yew betta do what she sez," the President said in a thick Georgia-accent, that came through a slit cut in the plastic mask's wide toothy grin.   "She vaporized ma brotha, Billy, and kidnapped me from the Oval Office.   Course, po' Billy only needed a spark to go up."

Jerome bowed to them both.   He was just dressed in a white shirt and blue jeans.   He hadn't thought to get a costume.   After all, the Apartment was his costume tonight.

"Right this way, Queen of the Galaxy, we have Venusian nectar on ice.   And peanuts and beer, Mr. President."

"You can call me Jimmy."

The guests took two steps into the Apartment and stopped.   Stopped moving, stopped talking, and briefly stopped breathing.

"Holy shit, Jerry," Jimmy Carter said, losing his accent entirely and lifting his face up so he wore the mask like a hat, revealing a cappuccino-colored face below.   "This is..."

"Freaky," the green-skinned woman finished for him, grasping his arm.   They moved further into the Apartment like children entering a dark wood.

The door buzzer buzzed again and Jerry admitted new guests.

"Ahh, fresh victims," he welcomed them, two Can-Can dancers, followed by Bob Dylan and John Lennon holding hands.

They also stopped dead in their tracks after two steps into the Apartment to Oooo and Ahhhh.

"I love it!" John Lennon said in a high girlish voice. Farther inside, the Queen of the Galaxy and Jimmy Carter were laughing themselves silly, pointing at the Tell-tale Heart.

The door buzzer buzzed again.

***

The Apartment filled up quickly. In dimensions, it was basically now a railroad studio, 20 feet by 40 feet from bathroom door to front windows. The Apartment had never been so full before. It had never felt a party like this inside of it, bursting with energy and music and laughter and love-making (Bob Dylan and John Lennon hadn't stopped making-out on the sofa since they arrived, as if the tableaus of horror were an aphrodisiac to them). By midnight, party guests in a myriad of avant-garde costumes and guises were spilling out into the hallway and onto the fire escape. The Apartment did Its best to swell, to expand a few more inches to accommodate a few more guests. It was insatiable.

***

Still going strong at 3 A.M., even by East Village standards the party was officially too much. Angry neighbors, upstairs, downstairs, and even from across the street called the cops who finally shut it down at 4 A.M. The responding officers had trouble convincing the crowd they were real god damn cops and not just in costume. No arrests were made even though the place stank of marijuana and spilled beer. Once they saw the set-up inside they understood how things had gotten out of hand. It was the 70s and this wasn't the first hippie art show they'd busted up. But even they had to hand it to this guy, Jerome. This was art they understood.

***

The Apartment liked these people, liked their reaction to It, and whether it was from the beer soaking into Its floorboards or a contact high from all the pot that had been smoked, the Apartment felt good, It was like before, when It was the favorite room and people loved It as soon as they stepped within.

By 5 A.M. everyone had cleared out, including Jerome who went home with the Queen of the Galaxy to her alien planet in Flatbush, leaving the Apartment vacant.

Its walls still trembled with the vibrations of voices and music. Its floorboards still quivered from the dancing feet. Its timbers still shivered with the pure energy and the wildness.

The Apartment swayed a little and the pendulum of the Pit and the Pendulum began to swing over its skeletal victim. Fortunato's face tilted forward, bulging red cheery eyes popping out through the aperture. And the Jell-O Tell-tale Heart throbbed and beat, throbbed and beat.

Gradually it passed and, as all apartments do, the Apartment settled down.

But the Apartment knew.

It knew It wanted to feel this way again.

For now though It was content to sleep.

***

When Jerome returned the next afternoon, his mouth, hands, and various other parts of his body were splotched green like a copper statue with verdigris.

Not bothering to shower, he put water on the stove for instant coffee, and while he waited for it to boil, took one last tour of his displays. Some of his best work, even though now in daylight it looked like crap again, Cinderella's crystal carriage now a rotting pumpkin. But he remembered how people had reacted and enjoyed it for a moment, before he got to work cleaning up. He took everything apart, breaking it down to pieces that fit in four black lawn-size trashbags.

He was a professional window-dresser, he wasn't someone who "put up decorations," he created unique artistic displays. But when he abandoned being an Artist and became a window-dresser, he embraced the disposability of his art, because in his opinion all Art was excremental and so flushable.

But it wasn't just his philosophy of Art versus Craft that guided him; space and the lack of it was a perennial problem. Often he salvaged things he could immediately recycle, but there was no profit in storing stuff, he had no room for it. Making the most of Space was a driving force in Manhattan, people connived and constructed to get the most of it: adding a loft bed to a kitchen area, making a walk-in closet into a second bedroom. Space was always an issue.

And again, his mentor Kent's sage wisdom came to bear: "Don't turn into a hoarder! You save something like it's your darling, think you're going to use it again, but you never do. Toss it! Or else what? Every year you're just putting up decorations. The corner drugstore can do that! And if so, why do they need US?"

At the time, Jerome's heart swelled with that inclusion of "us," but he also saw the logic behind it. Then Kent added a codicil to the pronouncement. "But also there is Tradition. I've got this ratty old chinadoll with a chipped left eyeball and nattered limbs which if I now didn't put in the Christmas display every year, Mrs. Macy's would cut my balls off. Cuz one year, I didn't and Mrs. Macy's cut my balls off. So now you'll see that every year til one or the other of us kicks it."

So after his first Haunted House Party, Jerome threw it all away, saved none of it. Except for one thing.

When he came to the opening in the floor and the job of scooping out the Tell-tale Heart, he chuckled to himself and just fitted the short key floorboard back into place and screwed it down, and left it like that.

He wondered what it would look like by next year.

Because without even knowing he'd decided, he knew there would be another Haunted HouseParty next year, knew he wanted to see all those reactions again, but with new horrors he would create that would make all the boys and girls laugh and shrill scream.

The Tradition continued for 17 years, and people often asked him, marveling at how much work he put into it, "Why do you do all this?"

"So, my dear," he always replied, "you will ask me why I do all this?"

Among the Lower East Side art community his Haunted HouseParties became legendary through the 80s, and 90s, an event anticipated and never to be missed, the thing you had to do on Halloween, the place you had to be in the East Village. Like most grand traditions, it just happened. It was the annual "underground" party that wasn't underground, everyone was invited if only they knew where it was, and often people just passing by on the sidewalk who looked up and saw through the window how wild the scene was, took a chance and crashed it. It didn't matter, since everyone was in costume, often Jerome didn't even recognize his own friends.

In that time, *ILL*usions (as Jerome renamed his window-dressing business) flourished and his work was always in demand; Jerome could pick and choose his jobs, but he rarely turned down any work. Except come every October first, when he began work on transforming the Apartment into the Haunted House.

Early on, one of the essential ingredients that made the parties "special" were the materials he used to create his *ill*usions: Jerome applied almost exclusively to The Sidewalk Gods of New York City.

It is a fact of the city that if you put something, like say a TV with a note that says "IT WORKS" taped to it, out on the sidewalk for collection, by the time you get back up to your apartment and look out the window, it will be gone. Like magic. An offering has been made to the Sidewalk Gods, and accepted. So that one day, when you need something--a pair of shoes just your size or a lamp shaped like an elephant--and you take a walk around, within a few blocks you will find just what you're looking for. It is magic.

So his Haunted HouseParties were built primarily from "found objects," what people threw away or left behind either through transience or death. They shaped the Apartment every year as much as Jerome's creative vision.

He never repeated the same theme, but over time some special effects were re-incorporated and people looked forward to his "Bottomless Pit" (he placed a 5x5 foot mirror on the floor in one windowless corner of the apartment and above it hung a wide black cone, which he painted the interior of with day-glow fluorescent paint, drawing forced-perspective lines--like looking up the skirt of a pyramid--that when lit by black light and viewed in the mirror on the floor gave the impression of a deep pit; some people even experienced vertigo, the illusion was so good), "The 13 Skulls" (he wrapped glue-soaked pages from The New York Times around a skull he'd picked up at a curio shop on 52nd Street for nine bucks, formed it to fill-in the eye-sockets and nose cavity, let it dry, cut the base skull out, filled it with cotton, and resealed it, then started the process again until he'd produced thirteen grinning skulls that he left unpainted, the news articles, obituaries, crossword puzzles, and stock quotes still visible in the light, but in near-darkness the newsprint became cracks and fissures in the skulls, and every following year he unpacked them, the newspaper got yellower and yellower and so did the skulls), "The Bloody Broken Window" (the frame from a torn screen window and along its inside edges he taped clear plastic artist triangles of different sizes and at different angles, but the final effect was shattered glass, that he liberally doused with fake blood and festooned with yellow crime scene tape, then fitted into the window that overlooked the sidewalk of Saint Marks Place), "The Clutching Hands" (two dozen cheap rubber hands that he glue-gunned suction cups to the base of and. then, at varying heights, stuck to one wall, lit from below with a strobe light so they seemed to clutch and grasp), and "The Black Curtain" (just a black shower-curtain that he hung across the combination bathtub/shower and each year something different behind it--once, a tentacle monster made of foam rubber and garden hose, another time just water in the tub and a crateful of apples bobbing on the surface--but it was up to the guest to go into the bathroom alone and pull the curtain aside to reveal what waited behind it every year).

And, of course, from the beginning, there was always The Tell-Tale Heart nested under the floorboards. Everything else he packed away every year and stowed it on the highest shelf of the Apartment's one closet.

No photographs exist of any of Jerome's parties. He never photographed any of them. He did try once but everything came out looking shabby. Brightly lit by a camera's flash, all the shadows and ambiguity were absent and it was just trash he'd dragged in off the sidewalk. Jerome's *ill*usions existed in the eyes of the beholders, what they "imagined" they saw when glimpsed in a certain light. He eventually came to understand that what he created was a photographic negative and the people he projected it on left his Haunted HouseParties the developed pictures.

Jerome threw his last Haunted HouseParty in October 1995. Nobody knew it was his last, not even Jerome, and least of all, the Apartment.

On the morning of May 3, 1996, Jerome Schwartz left the Apartment at 10 A.M. An hour later he died at work at the age of 51 of a heart attack while installing a Summertime display-window at Sac's. It was an outdoor patio set-up. He'd laid down a roll of Astroturf, when suddenly he felt queer. Indigestion, he thought. He sat down on one of the blue-striped chaise lounges and quietly died. For a long time, people thought he was asleep. Those who walked by on the sidewalk and noticed, just smiled and walked on, but other than that he didn't make a display of himself.

And he never returned to the Apartment.

CHAPTER FOUR:

THE BROKEN WINDOW

The Apartment didn't really notice Jerome's absence. For one thing, over the years he'd been gone for extended periods of time before--vacations abroad or shacking up with a broad--so there was nothing unusual about the Apartment being empty, and It welcomed the vacancy, the break from activity, the dust settling.

And for another, it was Summer, so Halloween was still months away, and the Apartment was content to lie dormant until It sensed the coming of Fall, asleep, and in Its hibernation, It dreamt.

The Apartment dreamt It was the size of the room It had been, but now Its walls were lined with every ILLusion Jerome had ever created, and into It came astronauts and nuns, clowns and bellydancers, Laurel and Hardy, Charles Manson, a hotdog in a bun, every guest who'd ever come to one of the parties, all come together, all at once, and the Apartment swelled to hold them. It dreamt It was the Haunted House, never-ending, all year long.

It wasn't until mid-July that it stirred and took notice. A key was turning in the hallway door's lock, the deadbolt was turned. The Apartment door swung open.

He's back.

But he wasn't.

Two squabbling men came in, who both looked a little like Jerome, but one was bald and the other fat. The fat one held the door open while the bald one kicked and carried empty cardboard boxes into the Apartment.

They started putting objects from the tables and the cabinet shelves into these boxes, never ceasing their squabbling. The word "you" was used a lot in many contexts.

They spent three hours boxing up all of Jerome's belongings, then left with the boxes piled in the center of the room. Four days later, two other man came, they didn't look like Jerome and they didn't squabble. They propped open the Apartment's door with a block of wood. They lifted the furniture--a couch, a table, an easy chair--off the Apartment's floor and carried them out into the hallway, and from there, down the stairs, out the front door, and into the back of a moving van. They did the same with the cardboard boxes. The futon they rolled up and left on the sidewalk along with a lamp without a shade and a coat rack. Within moments, they were gone, collected by three different passers-by.

The last things they took out were trashbags filled with the spoiled food and drink from the refrigerator, which they unplugged before they left. They locked the door behind them.

Apartment Five stayed like that, stripped to Its floor. It missed the hum of the refrigerator.

It missed Jerome.

The Apartment didn't understand.

In early September, a man unlocked the door. He came in dressed in coveralls and carrying a dropcloth and cans of paint. He gave the Apartment a fresh coat of eggshell white, slathering it on everywhere, wall and molding, and he refolded the shutters into the recess of the walls and painted them shut again. The Apartment didn't mind, easily undone.

A week later a new tenant moved in. An old woman, but not like the old women the Apartment had known, this one was stocky, as broad in the hips as the shoulders, with a head like a bucket. She had a lot of furniture and rugs and pictures that she hung on nails she pounded into Its walls.

She lived alone and was quiet, except when she spoke on the telephone, then she shouted in a language from another country.

She lived mainly on a diet of boiled cabbage. Again with the cabbage.

Other than that, she was a clean old woman of quiet habits, who went to bed every night at nine and arose at exactly six A.M. every morning, without an alarm to wake her, just her internal clock.

The Apartment didn't mind her. It paid little attention to her, It had had worse tenants. This one was no trouble.

The trouble began about Columbus Day weekend. The leaves had begun to turn. A fresh crisp bite was in the air. Morning's frost on the Apartment's windows. The slant of sunlight across Its floor was different. The Apartment's internal clock told It to wake up, October again, soon it would be...

A faint tenseness constricted Its floorboards and made them tremble and creak like when a garbage truck thunders by outside, but no truck had passed. The Apartment had shivered, not knowing why but sensing something was wrong.

It pinpointed the problem: everything inside It was the same. There should have been more activity going on. Furniture should have been moved to one side of the room, to make room for guests and decorations. And where were the decorations? Why wasn't the old woman building them? She was cutting things close, how would she be ready by Halloween? If there were no decorations, there would be no party, and if there was no party, there would be no guests.

It didn't understand why this was happening, but It knew this was unacceptable.

***

Mrs. Boroske had moved into Apartment #5 in September after vacating the apartment she and her late husband had occupied on East Fifth Street--three blocks over--for 14 years. Roethke Realty, the landlords decided to turn her old residence into a condominium and bought out all the tenants and relocated those who accepted to apartments in other buildings they owned and managed. Mrs. Boroske had been the last to agree, holding out for the most amount of money. But still she felt cheated.

This new apartment was too small, it barely fit all her furniture. Her neighbors were too loud, too young, too dark-skinned, always someone shouting and laughing as they went up the stairs, and at all hours. And there was never any hot water. And a cold draft seeped up through the cracks in the floorboards she could feel even through her rug. She hated the apartment.

Every night before she went to bed, she called up her sister living in that nice apartment in Stuyvesant and told her--in their native tongue--how much she hated the apartment, and couldn't she get her a place over there? Halloween was no different, only she could add the complaint of the noise in the street--the howling and car horns beeping--and how it would go on like that all night. How was she to sleep?

On October 31, 1996, Mrs. Boroske was in bed by 9 P.M. as usual. She lay under the covers, speaking to her dead husband in her head, berating him, blaming him for dying and leaving her to cope alone, he'd never had consideration for others, always been selfish--if her late husband heard her, he got an earful.

A sound at her window. She stiffened in bed.

A scrape--no, a creak, a pop! Someone was breaking in!

She turned on her bedside lamp and reached for her telephone.

The sounds stopped.

The shades on her windows were drawn down, but streetlights glowed dull orange on them and no shape was cast through their thin paper, just the flickering shadows from the tree branches outside. Had it been a branch?

Both windows shades spun up at once and Mrs. Boroske screamed.

Her eyes shot from one window to the other and back again, expecting to see someone crouching outside. But there was nothing. The empty fire escape through one. The branches of the tree through the other.

She forced herself to take a breath.

Her heart thumped against her chest, her ribcage ached from the force of it. She could hear it beating, feel it shake her whole bed.

She took a deeper breath and held it.

But the beating of her heart became louder.

She put her hand to her chest, ordered herself to calm down.

But the beating became louder.

And the rhythmic shaking of the bed like a raft heaving on a wave.

It wasn't her heart, someone was under her bed!

She threw back the covers and jumped out of bed, running to the window just to get away from whatever IT was.

As she got close to the window, her left foot fell into a hole. One of the floorboards had withdrawn from beneath her. She dropped down eight inches below the floor, crying in surprise as momentum carried her forward and her ankle snapped. She pitched forward off-balance, reaching out her hands.

Her palms landed flat against the glass of the window, She briefly saw her reflection, her heavy exhale of breath on the glass before it shattered outwards and she with it. Out into open space until she rapidly floated down to the sidewalk.

Where she lay crushed and bleeding, finally getting into the spirit of things.

Then the guests arrived.

This year everyone came dressed as police officers, firemen, and ambulance attendants, even the women.

The Apartment unlocked Its door for them.

***

After a thorough investigation, the police put down Mrs. Boroske's death as a freak accident. They could find no other explanation.

***

The following year, when the next new tenant was found with her head in the oven with the gas turned on in the early hours of November 1st, her death was recorded as a simple suicide (if a suicide can ever be called simple).

***

The Apartment wasn't malicious; it's wrong to imagine It had a plan. What It had was a course, a course that had been set--inadvertently, but indelibly--by Jerome Schwartz through the success and repetition of his annual Haunted HouseParties. Once established, the Apartment had grown to both expect and demand it continue. It didn't want to kill people, it just wanted to have a party. Every Halloween.

And not all Halloweens ended in horror. In 1997, the tenants were a pair of college kids, two guys studying a Fall semester at NYU. And they survived their stay, but they also threw a kick-ass Halloween party that year. Nothing close to what Jerome used to put on--most of their stuff was store-bought--but it didn't take much to keep the Apartment happy. Some years were better than others. As long as the guests arrived in costume and there was music and laughter, the Apartment was satisfied. And It playfully added to the decorations wherever they were sparse.

After the college kids graduated and moved out, the next tenant was a Swedish diplomat with a temporary posting to the United Nations. When he didn't show up for work after the Halloween weekend and U.N. security personnel entered his apartment and found him drowned--fully clothed--in the bathtub. It was assumed he was drunk, but because of his diplomatic status, his body was shipped back to Sweden without an autopsy being performed.

The Apartment existed under the radar for the most part. The tragedies that took place there were spread over time and their irregularity defied any official pattern to form. This was New York City and other addresses that raised more statistical red flags as the continuing scenes of violent death.

But long-term residents in the building knew, and they spoke of it rarely and then only to their fellow tenants, and they walked softly whenever they passed by the door of #5. Whatever was in there, they were just happy it left them alone, stayed where it was, and didn't spread through the rest of the building.

And of course, the landlords knew.

What they knew, they didn't want to know. Around the office of Roethke Realty (now Roethke and Sons), it was forbidden to talk about it.

Grace, their 50-ish black receptionist who had started working there right out of high school and now was putting two of her children through college, knew. She never said a word to anyone about the apartment's history, but if a nice young couple came in and smiled at her and asked if they had any available apartments for rent, and #5 was their only vacancy that month. She smiled back at them, God blessed their sweet hearts, then shook her head sadly without speaking a lie.

But this was Manhattan and the landlords couldn't just "not" rent the apartment, they'd be losing money. They compromised though. They didn't put the apartment on the market until after October, and then giving preference to tenants looking for short-term leases. Exchange students only spending a Spring semester. Or businessmen with temporary job placements...

CHAPTER FIVE:

THE BLACK SHOWER CURTAIN

The first new tenant who stayed longer than any of the rest following Jerome Schwartz's tenancy was Gerard Baldyga, who had transferred to New York City because his company opened a new head office in Manhattan. He moved in on December 1, 1998, so he had eleven months until Halloween.

His place of origin is not as important as where he ended up, Apt. #5.

The Apartment didn't care. It was used to people coming and going by then, and where they came from and went back to held no interest for It 355 days out of the year.

But let's say Gerard Baldyga came from Iowa and was 36 years old, single (never married), overweight but not obese, average height, balding since the age of twelve. He used to have lovely blonde hair as a child that charmed his female relatives and teachers, but now what remained--a cornsilk tonsure, wispy around the ears --charmed no females, or males.

Before he arrived in New York City, he was excited about his transfer, caught up in the rapidity of it. On November first, he'd been given a promotion and told he was to join the team heading up the company's new offices in Manhattan. He was pleased to have been chosen, never before singled out for his work. Within a week, all the details had been taken care of by his company--a pre-furnished apartment, a per diem moving expense, and an airline ticket booked and paid for--quicker than he could have imagined.

But soon after he arrived, his enthusiasm evaporated. His position in the company's new headquarters was the same as he held before, and the people above him were ten years younger than he was.

After a week, it dawned on him just how quickly things had happened, how he'd been caught up in a rush generated by his co-workers' congratulations on his promotion, their backslapping, their words of admiration and envy. "Wish I was you. You're getting out of here, doing something with your life." He hadn't really stopped to consider whether this was what he wanted to do with his life. But clearly it was what his bosses and co-workers back in Idaho (or wherever) wanted him to do. They were relieved to have gotten rid of him. Gerard had always been a drag.

His co-workers at the New York City headquarters took to him even less and more quickly than his co-workers back in Ohio had, and because it was Manhattan, they did not forbear from commenting openly and freely about how Gerard did not fit in. Whenever he entered the breakroom, their faces soured and they began finishing up their coffees and conversation and departing before he sat down. After the first month, it got to the point where Gerard developed a neurosis about it, which was the most metropolitan thing he did since his arrival.

He disliked New York City. The noise, the crowds, the speed of it. He fled work each night to get back to his apartment, and fled his apartment each morning to get back to work. At night he ate food that was delivered and threw the cartons out in the morning. He never cooked, never shopped for groceries other than milk for his morning coffee. He watched TV until midnight and went to sleep. He was a heavy sleeper--always had been--so even though he lived in the heart of New York City, the East Village, which only ever quieted down between 4:45 and 5 A.M., he slept undisturbed.

His life wasn't very different than it had been back in Minnesota. He'd had few social contacts back there, which made his relocation easier than it would have been for most people.

Time passed as it always did for him. Uneventfully.

Early on a rainy April morning, Doug, his manager, called him into his office for a work review. He was concerned about Gerard's creative output. Gerard nodded, said he was still getting the hang of things.

But both he and his manager knew: Gerard was out of his depth. But Gerard knew more, knew he'd been out of his depth even back in Nebraska or wherever he came from (he's soon to meet a horrible fate, so don't get too attached; not that Gerard Baldyga ever did anything in his entire life to deserve what happened to him when he drew back the black shower curtain, but neither did he do anything not to deserve it, wherever he was born and raised).

Early in life he'd learned to go along, give the responses teachers expected of him in school, and when that didn't work, mimic the work of others who did get approval. As long as he sat beside someone more inventive and creative than him he just assimilated what they did, and managed to pass all his tests, get average grades on his report cards, and eventually graduate high school and get a job that didn't require him to be either inventive or creative. He'd gotten by like that for over eighteen years.

But now he was in New York City and it was expected of him to be creative, not only in his job, but his lifestyle. His drab appearance and disinterest in social trends lead as much to his disassociation with his co-workers than did his lack of creativity.

He promised his manager he would try harder and he did. He tried to copy and assimilate his new co-workers inventiveness, but their ideas were too wild and when he tried to copy them, the results just triggered more undisguised derision.

Gerard's manager chose the Tuesday after the long Columbus Day weekend to give Gerard his second performance review. He hadn't wanted to spoil Gerard's weekend, nor more specifically his own, because it might've put him in a bad mood.

Behind closed doors, Doug, his manager, made clear to Gerard he wasn't fitting in.

He said, "Gerry, you aren't fitting in."

"I--"

His manager raised his hand like he was taking an oath, swearing to tell the truth, the whole truth, and nothing but the truth.

"I know it isn't your fault. It isn't that your work isn't adequate. It is very adequate, no one is questioning that. But working in New York City is more demanding and brings with it challenges you never had to face back at the home office. It's like you're a fish out of water here, Gerry. And I was wondering if you'd consider maybe it was time to get back to 'the water,' so to speak?"

Gerard had considered this already, done more than consider it, a month before he had called his old office and spoken with his former general manager, asking how they were getting along without him, and forcing himself to chuckle. The general manager was cordial, but before Gerard could broach the subject of coming back, he told Gerard how his replacement had settled in marvelously and she appreciated how Gerard left things in such good order to making her transition seamless. Then he told Gerard he had another call he had to take. But Gerard knew. He'd picked a time to call when he was sure there would be no interruptions. There was no going back for Gerard. Or going forward, he didn't imagine a glowing recommendation coming from his manager as he sought employment at a different company. If he didn't make it here in New York City, he wouldn't make it anywhere.

This realization hit him hard. He'd never had much of an imagination, but what little he did possess focused on the scenario of his becoming homeless, like the people he hurried by on his way to work in the morning and again later on his way home. It was one reason he didn't go out much once he got home to Apartment #5. It was the end of the 20th century and the homeless were everywhere in New York City.

That night, Gerard had a bad dream. He was sleeping not in his bed but in a cardboard box on the sidewalk, and the night sounds of the city coming in through his windows (even when closed) became the musical score to his nightmare.

He dreamt a drunk was pissing on him.

He dreamt a rat was in his pants, spelunking up his leg to get to his testicles and gnaw on them like ripe fruit.

A taxicab swerved and jumped the curb, riding the sidewalk, bearing down on him, tires on his head, crushing him into splat.

He woke from the dream in a full-body leap, his body arching upward from the mattress and dropping down again.   His heart pounding, he checked the bedside clock.   Only a little past midnight.   He dreaded the idea of going back to sleep, of dreaming again.   And then he heard a clomp.

***

The Apartment hadn't done it deliberately, It was just stirring, coming awake from Its hibernation, sensing from the chill in the air that October was here, well on the way.   It was like an underground sprout in Springtime shouldering its way to the surface.   All It did was shift slightly at its angles, but it was enough to disrupt one of the boxes of decorations Jerome Schwartz had stored on the highest shelf of the closet (neither his brothers or the movers had spotted them there) and it knocked against the wall and Gerard heard it.

Lying awake, heart still beating from the homeless nightmare, he turned his head in the direction of the sound and saw the closet door.   He got out of bed and investigated it.

Which is how he discovered the Haunted HouseParty.

It was neatly packed in six cardboard boxes of various sizes and dimensions, a couple of the bigger boxes were from Waldenbooks.   And what they contained made Gerard's eyes go wide.

If the items hadn't been so neatly packed and organized he might have been more shocked by the contents, but instead was dazzled like a man throwing back the lid of a treasure chest and beholding jewels and gems he knew not the name or origin of, but before his eyes lay treasure.

The first cardboard box he opened had a Chiquita Banana insignia on the outside and contained 13 severed hands, 6 left and 7 right.   Made of rubber and hollow, but painted so each hand was slightly different: one had liver spots and wrinkles; one had fingernails that looked bitten to the quick and soil-engrained calluses; three were the hands of children, three the hands of old women, two of them were matching left and right hands, both covered along the knuckles with coarse black hair.

On the base of each of their fake-bloody stumps were affixed suction cups, the kind that are kicked to adhere to smooth surfaces.

The reason for this Gerard only considered for a moment, then like a kid on Christmas morning, he dug further into the box to discover of what was beyond the next layer.

He expected feet, because of the hands, but not feet. Tarantulas, layer upon layer, 50 at least.

For a brief moment, Gerard considered the person who had stored these away, the man who had packed these all so neatly but somehow abandoned them when he moved.

The moment didn't last long, because at once he was opening one of the other boxes (this one with a Canadian Club logo on the outside) to discover SKULLS.

They were composed of old newspapers, the date of the issue could be read on some, October 17, 1979.

1979. No wonder, this was all some wigged-out hippies' party stash.

The newspapers were yellowed and cracked and despite the visible newsprint, in the dim light of his bedside table lamp they looked ancient, something excavated from an Egyptian tomb. The faceless faces stared at him without eyes, the vacant expectancy of their empty sockets begged him to pick them up. They were as light as balls of drying-machine lint, nothing to them but degrading paper.

Each of the skulls had attached to the top of their craniums wire hooks like the kind used to hand Christmas tree ornaments.

This time Gerard made the connection, these skulls were meant to be hung. It was as if the decorations were explaining themselves, "Here, this is what you do with us, this is how we work."

Lying at the bottom of the box was black plastic tomato netting, the kind his mother used to use in her garden to keep the birds off her vegetables. But here, in a different context it almost looked like black spiderweb.

Gerard saw it in his head like a flash, the netting hung from the ceiling festooned with the grinning skulls.

The idea of throwing a Halloween party took form in Gerard's mind. And his nightmares of being homeless ended forever.

When he was reclosing the box of skulls, he noticed for the first time all the boxes were labeled with index cards taped to their top flaps, taped with old cellophane tape that had dried and yellowed and were flaking off like jaundiced eczema.

So before opening any of the others (it was close to 2 A.M. now, but he hardly noticed), he read the index card descriptions first, so inside a box labeled "Entrails & Viscera" he wasn't surprised to find life-like human intestines, some with signs of chewing and decomposition, others that looked fresh, not just preserved but recent. Some sort of foam-rubber he guessed, he didn't feel like touching any of them that night. If he hadn't known from reading the labels on the box, he would have been more startled, maybe even afraid--it all looked so real, it was all so impressive, so...

Creative.

That's when the idea of throwing a Halloween party became solid.   Inviting Doug his manager and all of his co-workers and showing them he was creative in ways they could never imagine.   Because he could never have imagined creating any of the things in these boxes and he was willing to bet none of them could've either.

He explored further into the closet and the high shelf and reached for a box that was long and narrow and light in weight, except when he pulled it down a floppy flabby weight shifted inside it, to the back.   It was heavier than he thought or else it was caught on something.   Gerard had to tug to get it down.

It came free unexpectedly and knocked him backward.   Off-balance, he landed on his ass, the box on his chest.   Except now it felt so light, almost empty as he lifted it up and tilted it back and forth. Something inside slid back and forth.

The flaps of the cardboard box were folded over in a swastika pattern and on the index card taped to it was printed: BLACK SHOWER CURTAIN, and nothing more.

Gerard got up on his knees and opened the flaps of the box that were folded like a swastika, not knowing what he would find on the inside.

Inside was a latex shower curtain, black, still in its original packaging, with a square price label on it from Woolworth's.   69 cents.

The cellophane package was open, but the shower curtain had either never been taken out or else been carefully refolded and replaced.   Other than this though, the rest of the box was empty.   It puzzled Gerard, he couldn't see the horror of it.

Then he laughed at himself.   This wasn't one of the Halloween decorations at all, it was just what the label said, a shower curtain and nothing more, stored on the shelf with the other boxes.

The funny thing was, he needed a shower curtain for the bathroom's combination bathtub/shower stall and had never gotten around to buying one. He'd never liked taking baths (thought it was like stewing in your own filth). He preferred showers, but without a shower curtain it meant his bathroom floor was a swampy mess when he left every morning. Dark stains of mildew were beginning to form in the cracks and corners of the tiled floor.

He could have just gone to the nearest Duane Reade and bought a shower curtain, but Gerard didn't like to shop, invariably in his haste to get in and out of any store he quickly bought the wrong thing--the wrong size, the wrong shape, an incompatible screw-- so he had put off buying a shower curtain for 9 months.

But now, his procrastinations, his indecision, his phobia of being wrong yet again, had paid-off! Here he had a FREE shower curtain that looked good as new, courtesy of the previous tenant. And since he found it here it must be both the right size and right shape to fit his shower/bathtub.

He put the box aside and reached out to explore another box, this one labeled Christmas tree lights. Which is what it contained, but all the bulbs were red. Another box was labeled FAKE KNIVES and held knives that looked incredibly real and lethal, the edges nicked, the blades caked with hair and gore, but when he picked one up and flexed the blade it bent like a licorice stick. It made him giggle a little; if he hadn't touched it and tested it he never would have believed how harmless it really was. A prop and nothing more.

The next box, bigger than all the others, was square, perfectly square, a cube, and the sides of it were blank, no banana, liquor, or bookstore logo on it, just the index card taped on the flap and written on it:

11 HEADS

2 Blond Male, 2 Blond Female, 1 Redhead Female

3 Negro Afro (2 Male, 1 Female), 2 Bald Male, 1 Other

He poked around inside the box just enough to confirm that, like the others, what it contained was of unnervingly realistic workmanship, and above all: Impressively creative. He reclosed the box without digging down deeper into it to find out what "1 Other" meant.

One last box remained lodged in the back corner of the closet's upper shelf. It was another liquor box, Cutty Sark. He didn't know what kind of liquor that was, Gerard didn't drink alcohol, never did; his mother begged him to swear he'd never drink like his father did, and Gerard had swore to her he never would. He could see her swollen bloody split lips now, foamy pink spittle flecking his face as she begged him to swear.

Gerard came back to himself, realizing he was sitting cross-legged (Indian-style they called it when he was in grade school) on the floor half in the closet, half out, with the box in his lap unopened. He didn't know how long he'd been sitting there, reminiscing about something that had happened 100 miles away 30 years ago. Lack of sleep was catching up with him, he was feeling logy, it was past 3 A.M.

The index card taped on the box in his lap simply read GHOSTS. Gerard hesitated to open it. Not because he believed in ghosts, he never had; nothing supernatural had ever enlivened his imagination, not even as a child. Back then the horrors of real life reigned supreme, his father's drunken rage, his mother's bruised and swollen face. He shook his head to clear away the images. He hadn't thought about his childhood in decades, believed the deaths of his parents had closed that chapter in his life and there was no need to ever revisit it.

Still he hesitated to open the box marked GHOSTS, remembering the myth of Pandora and how she'd released all the horrors into the world because she wanted to see what was in the box.

Gerard unfolded the flaps.

Nothing sprang out.

All that was inside were clear plastic garbage bags that had been stressed and stretched and torn along the bottom edges into the shape of cartoon ghosts. He pulled one out. Microfilament fishing line was tied to the top. He held the ghost up by the line like a puppet and played it back and forth in front of him, the wispy plastic floated on the breeze he created. He found the motion peaceful, gentle, not a bit scary.

He carried it back to his bed with him, riding it across the air. He laid it beside his pillow, and then finally went back to sleep just as the dawn of a new day was breaking outside the Apartment's windows.

He awoke Wednesday feeling better than he had in months, better than he had in years in fact. He'd overslept a little and had to skip his morning shower, but he still went to work feeling fresh. He passed a homeless man begging for change at the subway station entrance without a qualm of dread or disgust, because now he knew that would never be him. Now he had a plan.

His co-workers noticed the change in him, for one thing he was smiling. His manager Doug, who'd half-expected Gerard to hand in his resignation after their talk, was surprised by his hearty "Good morning, Doug."

Doug's last name was a name Gerard couldn't pronounce correctly because there was a W and C and Z all together with an E before the I and double J. and the first time they met and Gerard stuck out his hand, he said, "Nice to meet you, Mr. jJrxoizAWoCZKeitch."

Doug winced at the mispronunciation of his family name, but smoothed it into a welcoming smile.

"Please, Mr. Baldeagle, call me Doug," Doug insisted, less to invite familiarity than to never have to hear Gerard Baldyga mangle his proud family name again.

"Oh, and call me, Gerard," Gerard said.

"Excellent. We're excited to have you on board, Gerry," Doug had said. "We're eager for you to give us the 'grassroots' perspective of the company."

Those were the most words they exchanged before his two performance reviews, but the morning of October fourteenth, Doug sensed a difference. It put him on guard, triggered a memory from his training. Prior to taking over his position as the company's executive branch headquarters manager, Doug had attended special training seminars to acquaint him with obstacles and challenges he would face. One of these seminars was: Recognizing the Disgruntled Employee.

Gerard's change in manner was one of the flags they warned about and circled during the power point presentation. Response: Engage the employee in dialogue, stress your interest in their well-being.

"How are you doing this morning, Gerry?

"Great, Doug."

"That's great, Gerry."

"Oh, Doug," he said, nonchalantly, "thanks for talking things over with me yesterday. Made me think."

"Not a problem, Gerry. My job."

"Made me think back to when we first met, how you were expecting me to bring some of the grassroots perspective from the home office here to New York City."

Doug nodded, it sounded like the kind of thing he might've said.

Gerard acknowledged that he had been having difficulties adjusting to his new environment. "Being a fish out of water and all," he said, chuckling, "so it's made me reluctant to 'let my hair down.'" Gerard paused here, then smiled to let Doug know he was poking fun at his own baldness.

Doug smiled back, and held his smile locked in place, waiting to see where Gerard was going with this and hesitating to break eye-contact.

Gerard launched into his fallacious explanation of the Halloween Parties he used to put on for his co-workers back home, how it gave a chance for everyone to get to know each other outside the work environment. Gerard was proud of this invention, but he'd been inspired, embolden, by the treasure he'd discovered in the Apartment's closet.

There were a few seconds pause as Gerard waited, feeling like a con man who'd just made his pitch, afraid Doug wouldn't fall for it, afraid his transparent ploy was just that "transparent." It would be seen through.

Doug saw through it, a pathetic bid for acceptance from a person on his way out. It was crystal clear.

He nodded.

Doug was no fool. He felt sorry for Gerard, but the man was already scheduled to be replaced. He'd begun interviewing applicants the previous week.

But he was also sensitive to Gerard's reaction to all this. If he complained that his attempts to bridge the gap with his co-workers was rejected, it would reflect badly on the whole branch and on Doug himself as the man in charge.

One way or another, Gerard's days at the company's headquarters were numbered, Doug had already sent the e-mail explaining the situation to his boss, basically arguing, We tried, but he's a drag.

But Doug reasoned it would be better for everyone concerned if they demonstrated how willing they'd been to make Gerard feel welcome, regardless of how things turned out.

He gave Gerard a warm smile and said he thought that was a great idea, he was looking forward to it. He would pass the word around, make sure everyone knew, and he AND his wife would definitely be there.

***

In Gerard Baldyga's defense, he truly believed his plan would work, his co-workers would be impressed by the creativity of his party and come to accept him as one of their own. Mass-slaughter was the furthest thing from his mind. He had no idea he had already lost his job and there was nothing he could do to change it (later, of course, police theorized that Gerard did know in advance about his upcoming dismissal). He was blissfully ignorant, so hopeful and enthusiastic to get back to the apartment that night after work and start putting up the decorations.

The first thing he put up wasn't even really one of the decorations, it was the black shower curtain, and simply because he wanted to take a shower. He'd skipped his morning shower and still felt the tackiness of the dried cold sweat in the small of his back and his groin from his nightmares the night before, A relaxing shower was just what he needed.

A rod with rings was already extended across the length of the tub, fitted into brackets in the tile walls just above the height of the shower nozzle.   It was just a matter of hooking the curtain to the rings.

The black vinyl smelled brand new as he unfolded it and shook it out to its full length and breadth.

Once hung, it dimmed the bathroom because the one light in there was a bare bulb in a fixture above the bath.   The black curtain cut-off light to the rest of the bathroom.

Gerard got undressed and started the water flowing from the shower nozzle.   Once steam was rising, he stepped naked into the tub and drew the curtain closed behind him.   The bathroom wall tiles were as pink as the inside of a kitten's mouth.

The water was just the right temperature and felt good cascading over his body, but his enjoyment was hampered by the odd sensation of isolation the black shower curtain gave him.   Completely opaque, there was no way to see beyond it.   He was used to showering without a curtain and, though it sopped the floor with the run-off spray, he was able to see the whole bathroom when he showered and see that it was empty.

And of course, it was empty now.   He lived alone, there was no one else in the apartment, there couldn't be, he had locked the door.

Or had he?   It was an action he usually performed unconsciously, so couldn't swear to it.   And if he had forgotten this one time, the door to the apartment was open and anyone could just walk in.   How would he know?   He couldn't hear anything above the sound of rushing water, not the door opening and closing, not footsteps, not the creak of the creaky floorboards--he wouldn't know anyone was in his apartment until a hand grasped the edge of the shower curtain and flung it aside. He was naked, exposed, vulnerable to attack, and defenseless.

The shower curtain wafted in as if propelled by a sudden short breeze and touched the small of his back. He shrunk away from it.

Had he opened one of the windows? Was someone coming in through the open window?

He turned off the water even though he was still lathered with soap suds, and listened.

A floorboard creaked.

That didn't mean anything, the apartment was always making settling noises, the building was old. Or it may have been a sound from the apartment above him.

The shower curtain billowed softly in again and he leaned away, avoiding its touch.

Gerard knew there was nobody in the apartment, knew nobody had come in, but he had no way of knowing he was right unless he pulled back the curtain and looked. He listened.

The shower curtain moved again, making a gentle susurration across the outer edge of the bathtub.

There's nobody there, he told himself.

Finally, unable to calm his apprehension, he thrust back the shower curtain. The bathroom was empty. He grabbed his towel and wiped away the unrinsed soap suds, then wrapped it around his waist.

He stepped out of the tub and walked to the closed bathroom door. A slight breeze from the crack below the door chilled his wet feet. But that meant nothing, only that it was cooler outside the door than inside the steamy bathroom.

He opened the door and the flesh on his arms started to goosepimple.

The apartment was empty. Of course it was.

He shuffled to the door, the door was locked. Of course it was.

The two windows were closed and latched. Of course they were.

Embarrassed, he shuffled back to the bathroom.

The black shower curtain was drawn closed across the tub. He couldn't remember doing that after he got out. Huh, another automatic motion, like locking the door when he came in, forgetting something he'd done without conscious thought--and it was wafting gently in and out, in and out, giving a mute imitation of mild respiration.

Now he knew there was nothing on the other side of it, but he couldn't see there was nothing on the other side of it.

The sucks and puffs were just caused by air traveling through the drain, and nothing more. The peculiar way the folds in the curtain shifted though, forming shapes then retracting them, reversing them, reforming them. The outline of a hand. The bridge of a crooked nose and a jutting clotted brow.

Gerard finished his shower by toweling off the now-dry soap suds which stung a little at the corner of his eyes. He toweled himself roughly and put on fresh clothes.

After that night he took shorter showers. And gradually fewer; the fear of someone lurking unseen beyond the black shower curtain while he was naked and defenseless didn't go away, it grew, so finally, by the weekend he gave up taking showers all together.

That night he moved his sparse assortment of furniture--the sofa bed and end table he'd bought from an IKEA catalog and had delivered, and the two chairs and table that had come with the apartment-- to one corner of the room. In no time at all it looked like no one lived there, just a bare apartment.

While pushing back the sofa bed he noticed a loose floorboard--shorter than the other lengths of slats that made up the floor--and when he stepped on it, one corner rose.

Examining it and putting two and two together, he understood the practical reason for it. The floorboard were fitted and slid into place, there had to be a shorter "key" piece in case the floor ever needed to be taken up.

He levered it up.

In the recess below he could see the striated plaster of the ceiling below between two 2x4 planks lying north/south. And a human heart.

It was nested like a giant misshapen egg in a black crown of thorns weaved from the stems of two dozen dead roses from decades ago.

Wires leading from it to a small white plastic control box with a switch that said ON and OFF.

He pulled the control box out. Carefully. It reminded him of playing the game OPERATION as a child, because he neither wanted to get pricked by the thorns or to touch the heart. It glistened with glitter and a clear plastic red-blue goo.

The plastic control box had a battery compartment on the back, with a Phillips-head screw that held it close. MADE IN CHINA was imprinted on it.

By the weight of the control box, there were still batteries inside, but how long had they been there? They must be corroded by now, frosted with a cluster of acid crystals. Expecting nothing, Gerard thumbed the switch to ON.

A sound, a whir, a creak, and the heart below the floorboards flopped once from the tip of its severed aorta, then kicked once from the bottom of its chamber. Flop-kick. Flop-kick. Flop-kick.

Must be Ever-Readies, Gerard thought.

He watched it arch and balk, thrust and retreat, surge and relinquish, expand and decline. He watched it beat. He wondered how long it would go on. Made a mental note to replace them before the party, but for now, he left the heart on when he replaced the loose floorboard. To allow it to run out.

With the room cleared, Gerard brought out all the boxes from the closet and began unpacking their contents on the floor.

Now here was the peculiar thing.

As unequal to the task as he felt upon unloading the plethora of decorations, the sense behind them became almost instantly clear and obvious. For instance, removing the black tomato netting and spreading it out, he found it stretched across the length of the apartment, and that at each of its four corner were brass rings. He considered it for a moment, and then noted that high upon the ceiling in each corner of the room was a corresponding brass hook.

He hooked one of the rings on, then the next, and then did the same at the other end of the apartment.

The netting formed a canopy over the room, and laced between holes were thin, stressed strips of black plastic from garbage bags.

With the white ceiling covered, it darkened the room, making the ceiling light--two 25 watt bulbs in a 3-bulb fixture--murky. Spindly shadows flittered over the walls.

The sag of the black netting made Gerard feel like he was under the wide bough of an enormous tree.

Then he remembered the skulls with their Christmas tree ornament hooks at the tops of their craniums.

He took one of the skulls and hooked it on the netting.

It hung low like strange fruit.

He unpacked the rest of the skulls and--spacing them evenly, but not orderly--hung them from the netting. The end result was a skull orchard.

It gave him a chill, how easy it was, and how impressive it looked, but above all it fortified his conviction that his plan would work.

Next he unpacked the hands, grabbing them by the wrists two by two; when he stretched out his arms he had six hands and it made him giggle. He laid them on the floor all in a row, as if they were on the starting line of a very very strange race.

It took Gerard a little longer to puzzle out what he was supposed to do with them though. Did he put them under seat cushions? Rest them on the mantle, maybe holding a glass? Everything Gerard thought of seemed kind of unimpressive.

Then he realized, the suction cups on all the severed wrists must have something to do with it. He looked around the apartment. The blank wall opposite where he had his sofa bed was brick-faced, but Gerard noticed for the first time since moving in, the bricks were somewhat shiny reflecting the light, not dull.

He got up and went over and touched the wall. A clear glaze had been evenly applied over the floor-to-ceiling bricks and long ago dried to a smooth non-porous surface.

He picked up one of the hands and brought it over to the wall, pressed the suction cup against it--and the hand stuck!

For a little bit, then gravity pulled it free and it fell to the floor, palm up.

He picked it up again, and this time--without really thinking about it--he stuck out his tongue and licked the suction cup.

His face scrunched up. He gagged. His eyes watered. It was vile, it tasted vile. He tried to spit, but his mouth was a desert. A spoonful of rank bile spurted into his mouth and he swallowed it back. But that at least cleansed the taste of the suction cup from his mouth. It was gone.

He wiped his tears away. Just to free up his hand, he stuck the hand's suction cup against the wall and it smacked against it with a solid, wet seal.

The hand reached out at Gerard as if it were coming through the solid brick wall. The effect was perfect.

He reached for another hand. And paused. He got a paper towel, wet it at the sink, and used this to moisten the remaining hands' suction cups.

It all came together so easily. It seemed so natural, he hardly had to think what to do with everything. And he'd only just begun, more boxes to unload, but already he saw the apartment was developing a distinct...what was the word? on the tip of his tongue...

Flavor.

The vile taste of the suction cup came back in memory.

Atmosphere. Yes, atmosphere.

One of the funniest decorations--if they could be called that--puzzled him because he couldn't see what was supposed to be scary about it: a life-size inflatable doll of a woman, fully dressed in the kind of frock made popular by TV moms in 1950s sitcoms. But the uninflated doll and dress were neatly folded, with the arms folded on top. When he tried to lift it out, it stopped halfway, didn't want to come out. Part of it seemed stuck. He looked under. The face of the doll was attached to a shiny metal grille at the bottom of the box. He lifted it out. The grille was the same shape and size as those inside the apartment's gas stove. He still didn't get the idea until he inflated the blow-up doll and instead of the legs inflating straight out, they were bent at the knees as if the doll were crouched or kneeling. Then Gerard understood.

He carried it over to the gas range, opened the door of the stove. There was an empty groove. He slid the grille into it. The inside of the stove was as clean as the day he moved in, he'd never cooked, ate only take-out. This was the first time he ever used the stove in any capacity.

The doll hung out of it. Gerard admired the effect: a suburban housewife kneeling with her head in the gas oven. The simplicity made him giggle again. He was giggling more and more lately. Maybe it meant, finally after all these years, he was going to be happy.

He tried to continue putting up the other decorations, but the doll distracted him. He kept forgetting it was there, only briefly but enough that when he glimpsed the figure out of the corner of his eye, it startled him on a primitive level: hunter detecting the presence of another, feeling hunted.

Eventually, he had to deflate it enough to fold it up into the oven (funny, his mom used to have a dress like that, but their house had had an electric range, so she couldn't do *it* that way). No fear of him cooking it alive before the party, he never used the stove. And it wasn't alive. Either way, it felt good to close the oven door on it and get back to work.

That evening he got all of the decorations up.

All, except for the heads.

He had decided to leave them for last because he still hadn't figured out what to do with them, where they were supposed to go, so he reasoned if he put up everything else where it belonged first, whatever space remained was naturally where the heads would go.

Except when he came to the end of the evening and all the boxes were empty, he couldn't find the cardboard box with the heads in it. Which was impossible.

He looked everywhere, but there wasn't really anywhere *to* look.

The floor was bare except for the other now empty boxes. He discovered that each box was slightly smaller than the other and they fitted neatly into each other like one of those Russian dolls, so in the end he had just one box with the others inside it. And this box would have fitted into the biggest box, the one with the heads in, except he couldn't find it.

He looked in the closet, the shelves were completely empty. He looked under the kitchen table. Nothing. He looked in the bathroom, even though he knew he hadn't taken it in there--he would have remembered unless he was going crazy--and it wasn't there.

He looked everywhere twice. Nothing.

I'm probably looking right at it, he thought, it's probably staring me right in the face. A trick of the mind, a blind spot.

He tried to put it out of his mind, but it was maddening. He paced the room methodically hugging the walls, only stepping aside to avoid the grasping hands, hoping he'd trip on the box or something.

The problem was it *had* to be there, there was no place else it could be.   He hadn't taken it out of the apartment, no one had come in, so it *was* here.   But he couldn't find it.

Unless he'd imagined it.   Dreamt it?   But why would he dream of a box of eleven heads?

It unnerved Gerard a little.   But just a little.

He had never believed in the supernatural and wasn't willing to concede to it now.   There was a logical explanation.   He would think of it eventually, but for now put it out of his mind.

[Spoiler alert: Nothing supernatural had occurred. And nothing the Apartment did either; the Apartment was uninvolved at this point.   No, the heads *were* staring him right in the face.   Gerard had absent-mindedly placed the box on top of his Westinghouse refrigerator when clearing the floor.   Just a quarter-inch above his line of vision.   Out of his sight, out of his mind.   Gerard would not discover this until the morning before his Halloween party, twelve days later, and during that twelve days he pondered the mystery of the heads' disappearance, unsatisfied, unrelieved, by any of the explanations he offered to himself, barring the supernatural or that he was going crazy.]

He fell asleep that night without difficulty. The eerie decorations didn't frighten him despite how convincing they looked.   He'd put them all up himself, he knew what they really were.   If anything they comforted him, like a row of stuffed toys on the shelf beside a child's bed.   He knew after everyone at work saw what he'd done here, what he had created, they would think differently of him.

The Apartment was located on Saint Marks Place between First and Second Avenues.   Most nights even with his windows closed, the sounds of the hustle and bustle of the East Village reverberated through the apartment--cabs, buses, drunks, druggies, howling crazies, all hours. And Gerard normally slept through it all, sounds didn't disturb him, he was a heavy sleeper. His mother used to say he could sleep through a war, used to say it on mornings when she was serving him breakfast with one of her eyes blackened and maybe another tooth chipped. She would ask him, in amused disbelief, "You heard nothing last night, Gerry? Your father last night? That didn't wake you?" And she'd shake her head and say, "Gerry, you could sleep through a war."

But those weren't wars he slept through, but massacres.

The point being, the noises of the taxis and the drunks never disturbed his sleep, they were white noise to him now. It wasn't the outside noises that woke him in the middle of the night.

It was the settling of all the things he'd put into place. Weight shifting, a balance disturbed, and one skull drooped lower, twisting on its stem, rustling against the netting. One of the hands slid down a quarter-inch into a comfortable, more secure position. A breeze from the shower drain--up through the pipes from the sewers below--huffed and puffed the black curtain producing a gentle susssss and sssssus.

All the decorations were making noise. So long cooped-up in those cardboard boxes--who knew how long?--they were now stretching out, unfurling. Not alive--just paper, rubber, string, tin foil, etc.--but breathing, so to speak. Even the boxes were making noise, empty of their burdens, now crammed inside each other back on the top shelf in the closet, getting comfortable again. All these little noises formed a chorus--along with one more--that woke Gerard from his sleep that night.

He didn't know where he was at first.

The first thing he saw was the black net canopy overhead and he thought he was camping out under a tree. He'd had to sleep in the backyard the night the police came and took his father away. His mother had already been taken away in the ambulance. He hid in the backyard and no one thought to look for him. He slept under a tree then.

He remembered where he was, what he was looking at. He heard all the sounds, the snaps, crackles, rustles, and creaks all around him.

And below him.

Flop-kick, flop-kick.

The heart below the floorboards. Its batteries still hadn't run-down, far from it. The beat was stronger than before, its gears more limber. Flop-kick, flop-kick, flop-kick. Its metronomic pace never varied. Flop-kick, flop-kick.

He closed his eyes. The sound became the only thought running through his head and after awhile he couldn't tell if he was sleeping or awake or in some somnambulistic state in-between. And when he opened his eyes the next morning at 7 A.M., he didn't really wake up because he hadn't really been asleep, but in a trance.

The beating of the heart was drowned out somewhat by the pervasive noise of New York City coming back into full motion, but Gerard still heard it and felt it, as if in the night his own heart had synchronized with it.

He skipped his morning shower. The idea of being naked behind the black shower curtain was unappealing. Not that being on the other side was much better.   As he sat on the toilet next to the tub, taking his morning dump, the black shower curtain kept puffing out, pressing against his face, touching his bare knee.   And again he fancied shapes outlined on the undulating surface, like there were people back there, messing with his head.   It certainly messed with his poo, he couldn't go, instantly constipated.

He found the whole apartment more unsettling in the daylight than it had seemed at night.   It was all revealed as tattered and stitched-together and grimy. The skulls, that had been grinning the night before, looked grim and disapproving now as if they resented the light that exposed them as yellowed, crumpled-up newspaper.

For someone who'd never had much of an imagination before, Gerard was getting a crash course in it now.

He didn't exactly hurry to get away from the Apartment that morning, but he ended up leaving twice.   In his haste he forgot the Con Edison bill he was going to mail on the kitchentable, remembering it only as he got to the hallway staircase, and had to go back.

He put his key in to unlock the door and hesitated. Wouldn't it be funny to find everything in motion? Spinning and writhing in a Cat's-Away-Mice-Will-Play frolic.   Like something from a Disney movie.   By opening the door now, Gerard would surprise it all and everything would freeze suddenly and look just the way he had left it.

Gerard swung open the door.   Everything was motionless, except what the breeze of the opening door caused,   a couple skulls turning slightly around to glance at him then turn away again.

He put down his briefcase to pick up the Con Ed bill off the kitchentable, then he left the apartment again, relocking the door, and heading for the stairs. And stopped again at the head of them.

He forgot his briefcase this time. Put it down when he grabbed the envelope. He had to go back.

He looked down the hall to the door of Apartment #5.

It will think I'm checking up on It.

He unlocked the door but didn't take the key out. He rattled the knob, then opened the door wide enough to take one step in and reach for his briefcase on the kitchentable.

And from the corner of his eye--
*

The Apartment couldn't help waking up a little earlier than usual. It was good to have everything unpacked and be wearing the Haunted House again. The Apartment couldn't resist taking a spin around Its interior, feeling the flow, admiring how It looked all dressed-up. It swelled and filled-out Its raiments. It was blossoming again. It could feel it in Its grain and every groove. Soon it would be Halloween. It strutted and spun like a Southern Belle admiring herself in a triptych of mirrors.
*

--Everything was in motion.

The skulls were waggling their jaws in mute conversation, like conventioneers at the first meet-and-greet of the season.

The hands coming out of the walls were twisting and reaching for each other, clasping in handshakes and slapping high-fives.

The stove door was open and the inflatable doll reinflating, unfolding, unfurling like a giant tongue.

Gerard didn't turn his head to look, that would be too much. It was only his fancy.

He yanked his briefcase out and locked the door again. He left for good this time, and wouldn't have come back even if it turned out he'd forgotten his pants.

***

He told himself he hadn't seen anything. Only my fancy. All the way to work, he told himself he hadn't seen anything. My fancy. Sitting at his desk that morning, he told himself he hadn't seen anything. Fancy. Around noon, his constipation eased and in a pristine stall of the office restroom--no black shower curtain billowing against his face or trying to cop a feel--he relaxed and his bowels released.

The relief settled his nerves. That's all it was just nerves. He was nervous about the party, but excited, too. If this was his reaction to the decorations--and he knew all their tricks--how would his co-workers react? How would Doug his manager and Doug his manager's wife react? Would they still think he was unimaginative?

Seated on the toilet, Gerard smiled. Hardly.

True, it was a lie. He hadn't really created anything, merely installed someone else's creative work, but they wouldn't know that.

But it bothered him a little. Now that he knew how it was done, he could be creative, too, couldn't he? Come up with something of his own, a decoration of his own to add to the rest. Then none of it would be a lie.

The black shower curtain instantly came to mind. It was spooking him without even being spooky, he couldn't even use the toilet anymore. But there was nothing behind it. What if he could come up with...something? Something scary.

He finished up and flushed the toilet.

Washing his hands, he asked himself in the mirror, what would scare him, and closed his eyes and saw:

The porcelain-white tub over-oozing with pulsating steamy American Chop Suey with eyes, hair, and teeth. Not Chop Suey but the offal shoveled off the highway after a massive three-car wreck, the unguent puree of tissue, blood, bone, muscles, and flesh, once a family of four, now ONE.

Gerard's eyes snapped open.

He'd have to think of something else.

He tried, but for the rest of the day that was all he could think of.

He worked thru lunch.

Gerard took his time returning home that night.

He walked the 23 city blocks rather than take the subway.

For the first time since moving to New York City, he felt the warmth of Manhattan. Here were people going into bars together, laughing, hailing cabs. Mothers pushing strollers and carrying bags of groceries. Couples holding hands. It wasn't all dirty and repulsive, it was just what you chose to see.

And even when he passed a homeless man who was building a fortress out of cardboard boxes in the corner of an empty FOR RENT storefront, it didn't seem distasteful to Gerard that night. It looked natural, like a bird building its nest.

He stopped at the $1 Slice shop a block away from his apartment and ate the slice there. He was hungry again

He walked home. From the street he looked up at the apartment's windows. The yellow crime scene tape impaled on the jagged bloody shards of fake-broken window fluttered in the breeze.

What must people think? he thought. Most people probably didn't notice, this was New York City, and those who did either knew it was a sham or believed that it wasn't. What would he think if he didn't know? And did he know?

Beyond the jagged shards, the apartment was dark.

He climbed the front stoop to the streetdoor and let himself in. Checked his mail, a Key Food circular advertising pumpkins, and then unlocked the second entryway door into the hallway and stairs. He climbed with his key in his hand, the only key he had in the world, to the only lock he could open, the only place he had to go, his only home.

He walked down the hall to the apartment door marked number five.

He listened outside it. There was nothing to hear. He heard more sounds coming from other apartments than from his own, a television blaring the regional nightly news with anchor Hugh Campbell, the clatter of pots and pans, something sizzling in grease.

He unlocked the door and went in. Switched on the kitchen light.

The Apartment was perfectly still.

In the glare of fluorescent light the decorations looked drab and stale. Silly.

What had he worked himself up about? None of this was scary.

It dawned on him just how important the lighting was to the effect. Brightly lit it looked shabby, but lit by just a few lamps and placed in the right locations.

Without even taking off his coat, Gerard began rearranging the four lamps he had in the apartment, two he replaced with lower watt bulbs. One he situated directly below the wall of hands so that shadows flung up to ceiling extending like cats claws.

It was past ten P.M. when he finally took off his coat, he'd gotten so involved.

He flopped down on his sofa bed fully-clothed and fell asleep with his shoes on, and for the first time in a long long time, Gerard dreamt of his mom.

She was in the kitchen, their old kitchen, and it was amazingly bright, white light springing up like a net from the crevices in the linoleum floor.

She was peeling potatoes at the sink while her double, her doppelganger, the gas-stove suicide victim inflatable doll was cooking at 350 degrees in the electric range, with the oven door open, of course. But he could see his mother's breath, it was freezing cold in the kitchen. She scolded him in white bursts, "Go out and play!"

He looked around the kitchen but there were no doors. He couldn't do what she told him to.

"Mama, I'm sorry."

Then the leg of the suicide victim with her head in the oven began to twitch.

His mother said, "That means it's almost ready. When the leg pops out like that."

He said again, "Mama, I'm sorry."

She didn't seem to hear him, or wasn't listening, tending to her stove, kicking the twitching leg, ignoring him like he wasn't even there. Or like she wasn't even there.

She wasn't there. He remembered. His mother was dead.

He woke.

Flop-kick, flop-kick, flop-kick.

It was morning again already. He'd slept fully-dressed, down to his shoes, like the homeless. This is what it'll be like when I'm homeless, he thought getting out of bed. Sleeping in my clothes so that my clothes are technically my pajamas and I'm walking around outside in my pajamas.

He went to work that day in his pajamas.

Work? What was that?

Gerard discovered that day he could sit in his cubicle from 9 A.M. until 4 P.M. staring at his computer terminal and do nothing else, and still they were paying him $35 an hour for it. It was a steal. He'd somehow forgotten what his "real" job was, but it didn't seem to matter. No one noticed or cared. He could go on like this for years.

His mother had crashed their car on the highway and run into another car that killed a family of four. Gerard was sure she hadn't meant to do that. That hadn't been her intention, she had merely...got... caught--

"All set for Thursday night," Doug his manager said, poking his head into Gerard's cubicle on his way back from the men's room.

"What?"

"Halloween Party, Gerry. Getting ready?"

Gerard smiled, suppressed a giggle (Doug his manager didn't know he was wearing his pajamas).

"Yes. Getting ready."

"Good."

At the start of the week Doug his manager had circulated an internal memo to all the staff--Jacqui, Lence, Patrice, Jonne, Petar, Robb, Heorgi, Khurfonal, everyone except Gerard--stating that while not a requirement it would be in the best interest of the company that everyone attend Gerard's Halloween party, and if they couldn't they should come to speak to Doug personally about it.

Doug took aside every member of his team to say privately, "Hey, as you know, Gerry, is on his way out, but he's eager to make this 'gesture.' and it's best for all of us, and for the company, that we 'gesture' back, if you get what I'm saying."

He was saying they all had to cover their asses.

They didn't quite get what it was he was saying, but they nodded and said they did.

In truth, they were dying to see where Gerard lived. Most of them lived in cookie-cutter high-rises on the upper East Side, like concrete gerbil encasements devoid of character but costing them a thousand dollars a month.   But Gerard had scored a great East Village apartment, and because they felt they belonged downtown more than he did, they envied him.

Gerard dreaded going back into the Apartment, but he had no place else to go.

As soon as he stepped inside, he felt it waiting. Not for him, but waiting for something.   Like it was holding its breath in a pregnant pause.   But what would it give birth to once it exhaled?

His enthusiasm for the Halloween party was dampened.   He had doubts.   He still hadn't found the missing box of heads and it never ceased to confound him. He wanted this to be over.   He wanted to cancel the party, say he had the flu.   He'd take down all the decorations and go back to how things were.

After Halloween.

No, now.   No reason he couldn't--

No.

--take them down temporarily.   Some of them. Just for the night--

No.

--then put them up again before the party.   It had taken no time to put them up, it would be easier the second time around. Yes, why not? What would the harm be?

The idea cheered him up.

He was lying on his sofa bed with the covers on him, but didn't remember getting into bed. His bedside clock said 11:13 P.M. He could have it all down before midnight.

He threw back the covers and got out of bed. He was fully dressed.

He turned on all the lights in the Apartment.

In his excitement, his haste, he flicked the wall switch to the overhead ceiling fixture too quick and one of the two remaining bulbs flared in a PLIP! FLASH! and he jumped--he was jumpy--leaving only one dusty 25 watt bulb remaining. Instead of relieving the darkness, it etched its contours more sharply and cast the shadow of the fixture's other two dead bulbs on the surrounding walls like carbon-blast residue.

Bulbs blew out all the time, he told himself, it meant nothing.

He started with the hands, figuring they'd be the easiest to take down.

He walked up to the wall, grabbed the nearest hand sticking out from it by the wrist and tugged.

It stayed put.

He gave it a firmer tug. Nothing, it didn't even slide across the smooth surface.

He pulled and twisted it. The suction wouldn't break.

He yanked hard.

The hand clamped shut around his wrist.

He screamed.

The hand yanked him forward.

The skulls overhead screamed like 13 steaming tea kettles.

Gerard's scream wilted in his throat, became wheezing grunts as he struggled, pulling at the hand, the hand pulling at him. A tug of war.

The hand was winning!

His shoes, planted on the floor, Gerard squealed as he was dragged forward toward the wall. Below him some of the lower hands were lending a hand, clawing at his ankles. One snagged the hem of his left pantleg in a tight two-fingered grip.

Gerard began to whimper and cry. Through his tears, he saw that at the base of the hand there was less wrist than before. The hand was retracting, sinking into the solid brick wall like a fluid surface, water or acid.

Gerard wriggled his grip lower, not wanting to come in contact with the rippling surface of the wall, but getting closer to it, almost touching it.

He screamed and let go.

And the hand let go of him.

Off-balance, Gerard shot backward and landed right on top of his bed.

The Apartment was silent. Silent except for the constant flop-kick flop-kick flop-kick of the heart under the floorboards. But Gerard didn't even notice that anymore. He lay in his clothes and within his clothes a film of cold jelly sweat glazed his body and fresh pee in his underwear. He shivered. If he lay still--absolutely still--long enough, he could convince himself it was dream. As long as he didn't look down at his wrist and see the livid four-finger-and-a-thumb bruises there.

But...

Maybe...

The novelty hands were more advanced, of a more complex design than he credited them for. Yes.

Inside them were gears and circuits and things and--somehow--he had triggered their motion. These Chinese, what would they think of next? They'll be the death of us

The hand did just what it had been "engineered" to do, nothing more.

It was Gerard's panic that made him believe he was being pulled into the wall.

And he told himself--had to tell himself something--there was another explanation, one that explained EVERYTHING. And it was simple. What was that, about the simplest answer being the correct one--something to do with a RAZOR, someone's RAZOR, occult's RAZOR, Orcutt's RAZ--

He had to stop thinking RAZOR. It was counter-productive.

The simple truth was Gerard was having a hallucination. And why? Because he was on a hallucinogenic trip. Because? The suction cup he licked at the base of the first hand he put up--and got that vile taste in his mouth--had been *laced* with Hippie Acid, LSD, Angel Dust, God knew what, but Gerard knew that was the simple answer. The RAZOR answer.

Stop it.

He had nothing really to worry about, it was all in his head. It calmed him down and he rested.

But he didn't get out of bed again the rest of the night, not even to switch off the overhead light and its one remaining bulb flickering now like a trick-candle on a birthday cake that the kid can't blow out.

He left the Apartment at first sign of dawn, dressed just as he'd come in. P.J.s to work. He arrived an hour and a half early, the morning of Wednesday October 30th.

In the light of day, the acid-trip explanation still seemed plausible, but Gerard decided it would be best to cover all bases. What if there was something odd going on?

He had to decide what to do.

He had to have the party, he was committed to it, no turning back. But after the party, he had to take down the decorations (IF he could) and get rid of them.

But would he be able to take them down? The idea of ever touching one of those hands again made his stomach turn. And his wrist ache (possibly he had suffered a minor fracture). In order to take them down, he would need some kind of tool.

He considered several options: a crowbar, a saw, bolt-cutters, a shovel, but finally decided on an ax. Not a hatchet, but an ax, one with a nice long handle so he could keep his distance.

On his way back to the Apartment that night, Gerard detoured to the hardware store on First Avenue and Seventh Street and bought a wide-bladed old-fashioned Fireman's axe with a two foot long red wooden handle.

He took it to bed with him that night and slept soundly.

He dreamt of the party and how it would be. How it should be. Like a scene from a Hollywood movie filmed in the 1930s. All his co-workers dressed in tuxedos and evening gowns, sophisticated and charming, sipping from cocktail glasses and champagne flutes. Laughter and music and three cheers for Gerard and his fantastical, magical, wonderful party.

He woke up on Thursday October 31st feeling great, better than he had in weeks. He peed in the bathroom and the black shower curtain was as silent and still as a lacquered Chinese screen. He still hadn't figured out what to put behind it. Zipping up, he decided to leave it blank. Just as it was, nothing behind it.

He went to his refrigerator to get some orange juice, took a long slug of it right from the carton. And tilting his head back as he swallowed, he saw the cardboard box labeled "11 Heads" sitting on top of his refrigerator.

Orange juice shot out through his nose. He laughed. Tears and O.J. streaming down his face.

There it was. All this time. Right where he'd put it--but forgotten he'd put it--when he'd been clearing the floor. Mystery solved.

The relief he felt was immense.

He had just been scaring himself all along.

He took the box down and opened it. He unloaded the heads. He placed them willy-nilly on whatever empty surface was available, two on the windowsill, five on the mantel, three on the endtable by his digital clock. Then the box was empty.

He was satisfied with the arrangement, but something bothered him. He counted the heads. Twice. Both times only ten heads, not eleven. The "1 Other" was missing.

He wasn't going to let it bother him though, wasn't going to make a mystery of it, to confuse him, trouble, make him believe in things that weren't true. Ten heads were plenty. Ten heads were better than none.

Gerard folded up his sofa bed before leaving for work, and laughed when it wouldn't fold up. He forgot about the ax underneath the covers. He felt so silly now, now that he'd found the heads and realized he'd just been scaring himself all along for no reason.

He tucked the ax out of sight behind the refrigerator. Out of sight, but this time NOT out of his mind. He wasn't going to forget where he put things anymore.

He changed his clothes that morning, put on fresh underwear and socks, a clean white shirt, and his best navy blue suit. He felt fresh and renewed.

***

Truth be told, though, much of this feeling was transmitted to him via the Apartment's own excitement, radiating now from every corner of it. Potent, contagious, infectious. It was finally Halloween and Halloween was a drug, and Gerard and the Apartment were sharing the same needle.

As he left for work, Gerard paused briefly at the door, turned back and waved, and said aloud, "See ya later."

***

The Apartment liked this tenant. He'd done a good job of decorating, everything more or less in its proper place, and the few mistakes he had made, well, the Apartment could tweak a little.

Or a lot. Depending.

So far though, everything was perfect.

***

Gerard felt much the same way. Even got some work done that day, remembering what it was he did. His co-workers poked their heads in whenever they passed by, "See you tonight." A couple of them-- Jacqui and Lence--asked if they could bring anything. "Just yourselves," he replied, automatically.

Gerard was starting to get excited about having people over. He had never given (thrown) a party before in his life. He'd never had enough friends to consider it.

At 3:30 precisely, Doug his manager poked his head in.

And Gerard got his first fright of the day.

"All set for tonight, Gerry?"

"Absolutely, Doug."

"If you want to take off early for last-minute preparations, I've got you covered."

"Thanks, Doug, that's nice of you, but I should really finish recording these contracts."

"Up to you. Oh, by the way--heads-up--the wife, bit of a health-nut. Into mystical, spiritual, that New Age stuff. Anyway. Only drinks white zinfandel and seltzer. You got that, otherwise I can make a stop myself at a wine store and bring our own?"

Gerard's heart skipped a beat. He said, "No, I've got that."

But it dawned on him: he had nothing. He had shopped for nothing. No food, no drinks, no refreshments to offer his guests. Caught up in the decorating of his apartment (and all it entailed), he had overlooked one of the basic elements of what having a party implied. He'd never thrown one before, but he'd been to a few back in...wherever he came from...and at every one there were bowls of chips or dishes of nuts or platters of cheese and vegetables with a dip. Plus wines and beers and bottles of liquor and mixers. And ice. Gerard wasn't even sure if he had ice.

He should have told Jacqui and Lence, YES, please bring something. Bring ice! Now it was too late. His mind was racing.

He poked his head out his cubicle, called to Doug his manager's retreating back, "Uh, Doug..."

Doug his manager looked back.

"I think I'll take you up on that offer, come to think of it.   Wouldn't hurt.   Like you said, a few last minute preparations."

Doug his manager winked at him

"See ya.   Seven ok?   Wife likes to call it an early night.   Health nut.   Haha.   Don't tell her I said that."

"I won't," Gerard said seriously.

Doug his manager was already walking down the hall again, thinking, "Poor guy, no sense of humor. Good to be getting this over with."   On his way back to his office he reminded everyone he saw about attending Gerard's little get-together.

Ten minutes later, Gerard was out of the office, down the elevator, standing on the sidewalk in midtown Manhattan without a clue where to go or what to buy once he got there.

A stoop-shouldered black woman was pushing a wire cart with three full grocery bags in it, and as she passed, Gerard had the wild urge to buy all her groceries off her for double what she paid.   But what if it was only baby food and diapers.

Instead he started walking in the direction she had come and on the next block he came to a D'Agostino's supermarket.   He trudged in like a wretched sinner seeking salvation in a church.

He got a grocery cart--happy to have something to lean on--and he began filling it with chips and dips, a tray of crudités from the deli section, some pre-sliced cheese, a bag of nuts, soda pop and seltzer.   And to his great relief, they also sold beer and wine.   He got a case of Heineken and three bottles of white zinfandel.

He spent $247.   He had to take a cab home, and once there two trips from the cab to his stoop, from his stoop to the bottom hallway, from the bottom hallway up to the door of Apartment #5.

He caught his breath before unlocking the door. Checked his watch, it was just past five P.M. Plenty of time. Disaster averted.

He opened the door. Late afternoon sun was streaming in through the street-facing window with the jagged shards in it and reflected off the slightly sloping floorboards and lit up the whole room with sunshine.

Gerard couldn't believe it.

The decorations all looked so phony to him once again. Just a load of trash. No one was going to be impressed by this! They were going to laugh at him. And no amount of white zinfandel was going to change that.

Oh my God, what had he been thinking? What mad fever had overtaken his brain that led him to believe any of this was impressive? It was a joke. They were going to laugh at him.

He sank down on one of the kitchen chairs by the door, the bags of groceries gathered at his feet. He unpacked the bags one at a time, opened a bag of nachos and munched on a few.

He put the bottles of wine and six-packs of beer in the refrigerator. He opened one of the Heinekens to wash down the Nachos. It made him feel less dejected.

So what? he philosophized, so what if it was just a load of crap, nothing to be afraid of. It could be worse.

He opened the oven, unfolded the doll, and with slow, sighing breaths he inflated it again and set it kneeling before the stove.

He opened the window beyond the "broken window" so the yellow crime scene tape fluttered like streamers.

The sun began to set past the roofs of the surrounding buildings and the streetlights came on on Saint Marks Place, casting new light through the leaves of the elm tree directly outside and new shadows on the walls as a mild breeze shook the branches.

Gerard sat down on his folded-up sofa bed and turned on his clock-radio. Tuned it to a local pop/rock FM station, Michael Jackson's "Thriller" was just ending. It was followed by Mike Oldfield's "Tubular Bells."

Gerard closed his eyes and sipped his beer and dozed, waiting for guests to arrive, while the Apartment made things all better.

***

Gerard's co-workers were not awful people.

By New York City standards, they were average.

They were self-involved, self-congratulating, self-helping, self-serving--they were young, not mean. By New York City standards.

But by unspoken agreement that night they were all going to Gerard's party to laugh at him behind his back. Not in a mean way, but just enough so they could have a funny story later on.

By spoken agreement, they'd all leave right from work and arrive all together as one. They speculated what it would be like.

"Do you think he'll make us bob for apples?" Petar asked.

"No, pin the tail on the donkey," Jonne said, and they all laughed.

Their mass disappearance remains a mystery to this day.

Later investigation uncovered that they all signed-out of the building together, at the same time, the eight of them at 6 P.M. Doug and Doug's wife were meeting them there later.

They shared two cabs down to the East Village. Their plan was to arrive early, leave early, then go home and put on their costumes for the real Halloween parties they were going to attend later that night, after ten P.M., when all the really freaky parties started.

They congregated in front and looked up at Gerard's building. They saw the jagged broken window with the blood-splattered crime-scene tape fluttering out. One of them laughed. "Looks like someone had an accident." And then they all laughed, no idea that was the apartment they were going to, not crediting Gerard for being that clever or creative.

They climbed the front stoop to the entrance door and one of them pushed the buzzer for Apt. #5.

***

Gerard sprang awake, spilling a little of the beer he still clutched in his hand. He'd only dozed off for a moment, but an indefinite infinite amount of time seemed to have passed. He wasn't sure where he was in the apartment, it looked different. He oriented himself by the windows to his left and looked to his right. The other end of the Apartment was obscured in a murky gloom.

The door buzzer buzzed again.

He stood up. The time! He'd overslept! What time was it? How long had people been buzzing. He looked at his clock radio. 6:33 P.M. He'd only been asleep a few minutes, but it felt much longer, deeper, heavier than any sleep he'd known, and utterly devoid of dreams, a pure black blank slate replacing all consciousness and awareness of self. A "Coming Attractions" preview of death. He blamed it on exhaustion.

The door buzzer buzzed again.

He strode toward the intercom by the door. It took him awhile to get there, he was still sluggish from his nap, but it seemed somehow further away. The floor had a more acute slant it seemed and made for a wider journey to the door. Unless he was drunk, but on only one beer?

He ducked involuntarily as something rustled and darted across the black netting overhead.

He was still looking toward it over his shoulder as he pushed the intercom's "door release" button without first asking who it was. He held his finger down on it, even as he heard both downstairs entry doors open and close, and voices in the stairwell, and many feet trudging up the steps. The buzzer reassured him that people were coming, other people would be here soon. He didn't care who.

***

The eight of them walked single-file down the narrow hallway from the top of the flight of stairs to the scarred and heavily-overpainted brown door with "#5" painted on it in yellow, the downward scythe of the numeral encircling the peephole, the Apartment's outer eye.

When they knocked on the door, the buzzer below finally stopped.

A deadbolt turned.

The Apartment door opened in welcome.

***

In unison they said, "Trick or Treat," even though not a single one of them was dressed in costume or even wearing a mask.

"Come in, come in," Gerard said, urgently. His welcome more a gasp of relief. "Come in, come in," (I don't want to be alone here). "Thank you for coming."

He held the door wide.

Jonne stepped in first, holding out a bottle of red wine to Gerard. He wore a wide bright smile on his tan Mediterranean face and it froze as he stopped and Patrice walking right behind him collided into his back.

"Hey," she said.

Gerard took the bottle of wine from Jonne's hand, the transfer drew him farther in.

Then Patrice, on her first step in, stopped, too, and Heorgi behind her bumped into her.

"Hey," Heorgi said.

Then he stopped, too, once he was inside. They each did, and their hallway chattering dampened to an art gallery's awed murmur.

With the last of his co-workers inside, Gerard reluctantly closed the door. He wondered briefly if there was a way to keep it propped open, so the hallway light streamed in, but he let it close, but didn't lock it.

Then behind him the laughter started.

Gerard's blood ran cold. Colder.

First, a girl's gasp that turned tumbled into a cackle.

Followed by a male's deep baritone, "What the fuh--" that spread into haw-haw-haw.

They were scattered about the apartment, broken into twos and threes. Khurfonal said, "Come look at this."

"Outrageous," Robb said.

Their laughter and chatter grew in volume. They started opening bottles and drinking. To Gerard's amazement, it all sounded...friendly.

Yes, they were laughing, but not at him. Their laughter wasn't mocking or snide or derisive. No, they were happy! Their mirth bubbled up in them like gurgles from a happy newborn baby. Their eyes were wide as they took everything in.

"How'd he...?"

"What....?"

"Wow, it's the Tell-tale Heart."

"That's sooo..."

Occasionally one of the women screamed, not shrieks of terror but fake bursts that ended in laughter.

One of the them lit a joint and started passing it around and the Apartment was filled with the old familiar smell of burning marijuana.

Heorgi and Petar were at the wall of hands making a game of trying to shake each one, like politicians at a rally. Gerard couldn't understand why they weren't scared of them the way he'd been.

Something slapped him on the back and he jumped.

It was Jonne. "Awesome job, Gerry," he said in glowing admiration.

"Absolutely," Patrice said. "You're so clever. Like Tim Burton."

"That's what I was going to say," Jacqui said.

"Thank you," Gerard said, it was all he could say. He couldn't believe it. They weren't mocking or making fun of him. They were sincere. They were impressed.

To his complete amazement, his party was a success.

***

WRONG WRONG WRONG.

The Apartment was insulted.

Where are the astronauts, the hula girls, the matadors, the werewolves and the Playboy bunnies? None of these people were in costume! They were just people inside It. They made the Apartment ill.

***

It should be mentioned that the Apartment had distinct in-bred expectations of Halloween that needed to be satisfied.

The Apartment had dressed-up for the occasion.

It expected nothing less of Its guests.

Nothing less.

It didn't matter to the Apartment how corny or feeble the homemade costumes might be--most of the Apartment's effects were corny and feeble--but the effort HAD to be made and the tradition respected. For the Apartment to be the only one in costume at Its own party was humiliating. Maddening.

The downstairs door buzzer buzzed on Its intercom. The tenant buzzed back. The Apartment felt new guests coming up the outer stairs. It waited on their arrival.

But if Jolly Ol' Saint Nick or Sweet Jesus or someone like that didn't walk through Its door, things were going to get ugly. Participation was a mandatory enforceable requirement with the Apartment on Halloween. One way or another: You came in costume or you

***

Gerard opened the door to find Doug his manager and Doug his manager's wife.

They were not in costume.

They were the last guests to arrive.

"Sorry we're late."

He handed Gerard a chilled bottle of white zinfandel and introduced his wife.

The party was getting loud and he couldn't hear her name over the din.

She had soft brown shoulder-length hair, a pale porcelain-like complex, and toffee-colored eyes. She smiled at Gerard, pleased to meet him, and her cheeks dimpled deeply. Gerard fell in love with her in an instant. Love at first sight, something he'd heard about, read about, but never believed in, like ghosts and justice.

She reminded him of a girl he'd had a crush on in high school. Cathy McGuirk. He'd never had the nerve to ask her out. Senior year she had a big party and he was one of the few people she didn't invite. She went to college and her family moved away--he never learned why--and he never saw her again.

This wasn't her. Cathy had been chunkier and this young woman was lithe and muscular like a dancer. But her face stirred memories and those memories muddied his perception and he saw Cathy McGuirk in front of him, attending *his* party.

"Welcome," he said, ushering them in.

The palms of his hands had gone sweaty and the doorknob slipped from his grip, just as a gust from the open window blew through and slammed the door shut. Cathy McGuirk had to hop out of the way.

"Whoosh," she said, laughing lightly. "I'm scared already."

***

Doug his manager's wife, whose name was Theda, was a Pilate's instructor, but remember, this all took place in 2000 and she was somewhat ahead of her times, a pioneer, and after her death /disappearance/ dismemberment/ dis*ILL*usionment, whatever it can be called, it would be several years before the craze truly caught on around the nation.

But she should've worn a costume.

***

Doug, his manager, was dressed as he had been at the office. Cathy McGuirk wore a loose-fitting Autumnal wool sweater and blue jeans and blue track shoes with socks that only went halfway up her ankles and had fuzzy blue balls on the back.

When the others saw Doug arrive, they called to him, "You've got to come see this, Doug!"

Doug went over to see, leaving Gerard with his wife.

Her big brown eyes gleamed and sparkled as she took the Apartment in at one roving glance.

"You must really love Halloween," she said.

Gerard smiled and nodded, content to have an excuse to make direct eye-contact with her. He didn't know brown eyes could sparkle like that.

"May I get you a drink?" he asked, feeling more suave than ever before in his life.

"Thanks, may I use your bathroom first?"

Doug came back from his quick tour. He looked excited.

"Honey, you've got to check this out. Gerard, I...this is truly... Don't know what to say. Good job. I'm impressed. Didn't know you had this...side to you, if you know what I'm saying. I think we've got you in the wrong department, man. You shouldn't be filing contracts. Let's talk tomorrow."

Gerard said, "You bet."

"Honey, come on, you've got to see--"

"--Just got to use the bathroom. Hold your horses."

Gerard showed her where it was. The door was ajar, but he knocked anyway, got no response and opened it wide for her. The motion caused the black shower curtain--fully extended across the tub--to ripple and rattle its rings on the rod.

He bowed and stepped away.

Her smile was so wide it made her dimples look drill-pressed.

Gerard opened one of the bottles of white zinfandel and was pouring some into a plastic cup and "The Monster Mash" came on the radio as a shriek cut across the apartment's length like a rocket. Everyone went silent. Then they all laughed, thinking it was just another Halloween effect.

Gerard knew it wasn't. He started toward the bathroom door with the bottle of wine and cup still in his hands.

The door flew open, banging against the inner wall, and Doug's wife backed out, tripping over her heels. She staggered back, never taking her eyes off the interior of the bathroom.

Everyone was silent again, except for

"Whad'eva happen' to my Twann-sull,wayne-yah Twist???"

Doug's wife backed herself into the wall, her clawed fingernails scraped the plaster. She looked so like a heroine in a grainy black and white silent movie--her skin squid pale, her eyes bulging, emoting, from their sockets--that they all thought she was play-acting. Nervously a few of them laughed. Someone clapped and she swung out of her fugue (stupor, shock) and faced them all.

"Fuh you da livin' my mash's meant tooooooooo."

Her gaze leveled on Gerard. They blazed with new life and glistened with tears. She took two uneven steps in his direction and said in a deep husky voice, "How...could...you?"

"H'ucku..."

"How could you!" she said.

"I'ke..."

"HOW!" She raised her clawed fingers and flexed them into fists. Her hands were so dainty, the fingers so thin, that balled into fists so tight they didn't look like hands but hand grenades at the ends of her wrists.

He backed away, sure she was going to hit him

"I'm sorry!" He didn't know what for, but he was sorry.

She didn't hit him. Stopped herself because it would have meant touching him. Instead she turned and found her husband standing dumbstruck with the rest and ran to him. She wrapped her arms around him, pinning his arms down, so his hands flapped by his sides trying to rise up in comfort.

"Honey, what's wrong? What happened?"

She was heaving sobs..

Doug his manager shouted at Gerard, "What did you do to my wife!"

Gerard still holding the bottle of white zinfandel and cup held them up higher as if to say I poured her some wine, the kind you said she liked, but he couldn't think of anything actually to say, with words. He'd done nothing to Doug his manager's wife.

Doug went back to trying to soothe his wife, get her to tell him what was wrong.

She took a long controlling breath and slowly let it out again, composed herself.

"The bathroom," she said. "Obscene."

"What do--"

"Behind the black curtain. The thing he put behind the shower curtain."

"I don't un--"

"I want to go, Doug. Now."

"Ok, honey, ok." He turned and looked at Gerard, said his name like it was an accusation and a demand for an explanation.

"Gerard."

Gerard sputtered trying to defend himself, not knowing what he was defending himself from. The bathroom? The shower curtain? He hadn't put anything behind the black shower curtain! Hadn't been able to American Chop Suey think of what to put behind it and just left it blank. There was nothing behind the black shower curtain, except a bar of soap. This woman was crazy!

He couldn't say all that. Finally he said, "I didn't do anything. I couldn't."

None of his co-workers were looking at him, they were all huddled around Doug's wife trying to comfort her.

And snap, just like that the party changed. Everything had been going so well--

"Caught on inna flash!"

--and now was reversed, everything good erased.

He said, "Look, I'll show you," but they were all looking for their coats. Gerard tried anyway, putting down the bottle and cup, he marched up to the bathroom door. It was closed again. And not ajar. Shut, even though he'd seen her leave it open. He almost knocked, but everyone was on the other side of the room. He looked back at them over his shoulder, none of them were looking his way, and he thought:

"Is this a trick? Are they playing a trick on me?"

Time stood still in the Apartment as Gerard raced to the obvious conclusion:

They cooked this all up, they were making fun of him, poking fun at him. They weren't his friends, none of them liked him. And they think because it's

Halloween they can get away with pranking me, laughing in my face not just behind my back.

One of them is probably hiding in there right now, waiting to jump out at me.   I'll scream and they will get their jollies.

He wouldn't give them their jollies.   He opened the door, went in, and closed and locked the door behind him.

"Okay," he said, no nonsense.   "Joke's over."

The black shower curtain answered him with a mild flutter.

"I know what you're doing," he said.

No reply, not even a flutter.

"Okay," he said.

He grabbed one of his towels from a coat hook on the wall, bunched it up, and threw it at the black shower curtain.

It hit the wall behind and slid down into the empty tub.   The curtain billowed back into place, swallowing it from view.

Gerard had had enough.   He flung the curtain back.

And the last thing he expected

Nothing.   After all that.   Nothing.   The pink bathroom tile walls like the inside of a yawning kitten's mouth, the tub white and empty except for the bunched-up towel.   He looked down at the drain, not even a hair.

He had expected something, a turd maybe.   But nothing.

The joke was on him.

They planned this all and got Doug his manager's wife to playact it. If she was even his wife!   An actress.   This was New York City, not hard to find an actress willing to help play a trick on Halloween.   She deserved an Oscar for her performance.

And that's why Doug and his so-called wife arrived later than the others, to give his co-workers time to set Gerard up, make him believe they were all impressed by what he'd done, pretending they all of a sudden respected him, liked him and wanted to get to know him better. All part of the prank--or what did they call it nowadays, punk'd.

And like the perfect fool he fell for it.

And they had him apologizing, begging, almost crying--he touched his cheek--crying, and making him feel like a *monster*. The way Cathy McGuirk looked at him, wanting to hit him. All that, just so they could get their jollies.

And what now? They're waiting out there for him to come out, waiting to shout "April Fools!" or "Punk!" or "Trick or Treat!

AND NONE IN COSTUME.

Exactly. Waiting out there so they can humiliate him, so Doug his manager can announce his permanent transfer to their Homeless division, effective immediately.

And they'd all laugh at him, laugh their heads off.

Laugh their fucking heads off.

They were waiting for him to come out.

Okay, he would come out.

He switched off the bathroom light.

Opening the door ever so slowly, he peered out through the narrow slit.

Laugh their fucking heads off.

THE FIREMAN'S AX.

Yes, behind the refrigerator. If only he could get to it in time without any of them noticing.

They were all still gathered in the farthest part of the room--somehow farther tonight--still huddled around Doug his manager's wife, calling their next play.   He opened the door wide enough to creep out and, hugging the wall, made his way to the refrigerator before anyone noticed him.

He reached behind for the ax--

THE FIREMAN'S AX

--yes, yes, the fireman's ax, got it.   It was still in the bag with the receipt in it, but it didn't matter, the bag was only plastic.

He dragged the ax behind him like a tail as he took a step toward them.

Doug his manager noticed him first, came forward first, spoke to him first. First come, first serve.

"Gerard, you--"

Gerard wished he had something clever to say, like "Ax not what you can do for your country," but he wasn't very creative.   Instead he shouted at the top of his lungs: "American CHOP SUEY!"

"wH--"

Gerard choked up on the ax-handle, gauging the distance perfectly, swung and buried the blade dead center of Doug his manager's forehead.

Gerard kicked him in the belly to dislodge the blade and the falling body knocked down three of the others.

Cathy McGuirk got hers next.   Didn't even scream this time.   Fakey!

Gerard screamed for her.

"American CHOP SUEY!"

Two down, eight to go.

The three who'd fallen down didn't get up, just scuttled crab like back into the corner by the cast-iron radiator.   They were next.   He didn't even worry about the others, they were too traumatized to rush him, their only thought was ESCAPE.

They circled around behind him then made a beeline for the Apartment's door.   But it would be locked. Gerard knew it would be locked. That door would not open again tonight.

He went at the three on the floor like he was cutting up slaw.

Five left.

They were all crammed against the apartment door, trying to get it open. The door wasn't even locked! Their bodies pressed against it prevented them in their blind panic from opening it. He killed one of them straight off, Kurfulnoodle or whatever his name had been.

The rest got by him, ran, looking back--the fear on their faces--ran for the only other exit they saw, the window.

His co-worker Robb got snagged by the wall of hands, eight of them closed upon him, two to an arm, two to a leg, holding him steady for Gerard so he got a good aim at the throat. Perfect follow-thru. Robb's head hit the floor.

There you are, Gerard thought, before moving on to the last of them, now things add up.

They were trying to get out through the window with jagged points and fluttering crime scene tape, no matter if they had to jump two stories down to the cement pavement.

But the aperture was smaller than before, only wide enough to get a hand through. They tore at the plastic artist-triangles but their hands met real glass that cut and slashed the flesh off their fingers in ribbons, gashed their palms to raw meat. And hard as they tried, the glass wouldn't break.

With their backs to him like that, the rest were easy.

*

On the sidewalk below, walking along Saint Marks Place in the direction of First Avenue, Burt Reynolds (The Bandit) and Dolly Parton looked up at the window of Apartment #5, attracted by the fluttery crime scene tape and the wild commotion. They stopped in their boots.

"Hey, y'all, lookee here!" Burt called out (she had a sweet Kentucky accent) to their companions, Darth Vadar and Princess Leia, who'd got a head of them. "Someone's having a helluva party. Let's CRASH it!"

"Some kind hardcore punk art show by the looks," Dolly said, in a deep baritone voice, but he didn't sound too certain.

"Oh my God," Burt said, "you guys come look! Ya gotta see. All the fake blood, and-- They must be filming a movie. You guissssssse!"

"We'll be late for the contest," Darth Vadar whined in a nasally voice. "Come onnnnnnnn."

"But--" Burt said. "Never mind. Over now anyway. But if they were coming to the contest, they'd win hands down."

Dolly Parton started telling Burt how he'd once seen Karen Finley smear her naked body with chocolate sauce on stage, as they walked on to their destination.

*

Flop-kick, flop-kick. Flop, kick. Flop...kick. Flop......k– Flop.

Gerard raised his chin from his chest, he must've been dozing. The coagulated blood on his shirt stuck to his chin stubble and he peeled it off.

What was that sound? It was deafening, echoing, never-ending steel drums. It was silence, the echoing vacuum of silence. The heart had stopped beating, the batteries had finally run-down.

Gerard sighed, he was grateful. He looked around the Apartment from his chair drawn up to the kitchen table, feeling like many hosts do after their party is over. Dejected, but also relieved. And now there was the clean up. He would need more trashbags. Many more.

First he needed a shower. He was drenched in blood and brains and scalp fleck and eye tissue, and god knew what else. It had been quite a party. He peeled off his clothes where he sat and walked naked into the bathroom. The blood dripping from him made the bathroom floor slick as a slippy-slide and he had to reach out his hand to steady himself. And when he removed his hand, the bloody print he left behind immediately began to disappear, as if it were evaporating or being soaked up.

That will make clean-up easier, Gerard thought, vaguely.

The shower was going full strength, steam rising from behind the black shower curtain. He pulled it back, sucked in a breath.

"hhH, I should have knocked. May I join you?"

No one there.

*

Gerard Baldyga was the main person of interest in the mass disappearance of his 9 co-workers and one co-worker's wife, since they'd all been last known to be attending a party at his residence.

When building management gave police detectives entry into Apartment #5 three days after Halloween, they found the place empty, only the furniture and appliances it had come with and the few pieces Gerard had bought. No signs there had ever been a party.

The investigation progressed no further, because Gerard Baldyga--white male, age 36, balding--had disappeared along with the rest. The main office of their company closed their Manhattan branch. It was speculated they'd all joined some sort of cult, and sooner or later they'd turn up.

The police never found any one of them.

Except Gerard Baldyga.

The police found Gerard a lot, regularly, two, three times a week, sleeping in doorways, on steamy subway grates, huddled in the corner of an ATM vestibule, eating garbage out of $1 Slice's dumpster.

Each time these crime-solvers found him, they said the same thing, "Hey, can't sleep here, you gotta move along."

And he and his collection of cardboard boxes would move on.

In Toody and Muldoon's defense, Gerard no longer fit his general description. He had lost a lot of weight. And his hair had started to grow back--go figure. If only he could bottle what happened to him, then maybe he wouldn't be homeless.

But no, best not.

INTERLUDE

Following the disappearance of the last tenant, Gerard Baldyga, and his ten guests who attended his October 31, 1999 Halloween Party in Apartment #5 (their disappearance never explained despite combined efforts of law enforcement agencies and the individuals' families, they were largely presumed to have all joined a cult and one day, they would surface again, because ten people did not just disappear without a trace), Roethke and Sons, the landlords of the building on Saint Mark's Place in the East Village, took the apartment off the market from 1999 to 2004. It was Roethke Senior's personal decision. His two sons could not budge him from it. He had been alone inside the apartment one day.

***

Once the ruckus died down--the cops had been in and out of the apartment and found not a trace-- Roethke Senior sent his main superintendent, Wasyl, to look the place over, slap a coat of paint on it, wash the windows, and then they'd put it back on the market.

Wasyl came back to the office. Said he'd need a couple more men. One of his fell off a ladder changing a lightbulb. But Sol Roethke sensed there was more.

"What?"

Wasyl didn't answer wouldn't answer, except to say, "More men."

Exasperated, Sol waved him out of his office. "The wife is away visiting her mother this week. I'll do it myself."

He said it to shame Wasyl, make him back down and change his tune, but Wasyl didn't change his tune. However, the idea appealed to him. Get a little exercise, get back to his roots. Painting, scrubbing, the honest working man's gym.

The next morning he showed up at the office, dressed in blue jeans and sneakers, carrying paint brushes and scrapers.

He poked his head in long enough to tell Grace the receptionist he'd be working at 65 #5 all morning.

Grace called after him, but he grinned and waved through the streetdoor window. He wanted to get an early start.

When he got to the apartment it was completely empty.

He sat down on the floor.

At 6 P.M., Grace started closing up the realty office. None of the Roethke Sons were in that afternoon, just Mr. Roethke Sr. and he hadn't returned since she saw him at opening.

Grace had to get home to her family, but Mr. Roethke Sr. was family, too.

She went to the keys cabinet and got the keys for 65 STM and for unit #5. She locked the office without turning off the lights and walked the two blocks to 65 Saint Marks.

She'd never been inside before. It was ordinary, in better shape than some of her employer's buildings. She walked up to the first landing and found #5.

She knocked on the door.

"Mr. Roethke?"

No response.

She put the key in the lock and turned it. She opened the door.

Sol Roethke, Sr. fell upon her. His hands dropped on her shoulder, but his face landed on her ample chest.

"Grace, thank holy God," he mumbled in her bosom.

"Mr. Roethke!"

"Oh, Grace, how...how..."

"Mr. Roethke, get hold yourself!"

"How long has it been?"

"Been?"

Sol Roethke never spoke another word to anyone about what happened in unit #5. But his mind was made up. They were no longer renting it.

***

For five years, the Apartment was off-the-market and remained empty and dormant.

It woke briefly on next October 31. Nothing usually disturbed the Apartment--car horns, sirens, screams were just the sustained utterance of New York City a throb--but It heard the happy laughter and sounds associated with Halloween on the sidewalks two stories below its front-facing windows. The battery-operated rubber-heart under the floorboards responded--flop-kick, flop-kick--like an internal alarm clock going off. Time again, time for the Haunted House party.

But as It resurfaced, refocused, and assessed Itself, Apartment Five knew it was empty, vacant. Not a stick of furniture. The refrigerator was unplugged and silent. Dust coated Its floor. Not a single crumb in the kitchen to attract a mouse or even a cockroach. For the first time in decades, the Apartment was alone on Halloween.

A pang struck It, quivered Its joists, shook loose a swirl of talcum-fine plaster dust.

The Apartment didn't like people, yet Its inherent function was to lodge them, settle them. At best, the Apartment tolerated Its inhabitants, but it was dawning on It they were an unfortunate necessity. They stunk. Worse their stink permeated into the grains of the wood. They violated the Apartment with their every breath and fart. Soiled it with their wetness, their many different wetnesses. Some people had peed on Its floors, and not just in the bathroom. It was degrading.

As much as It disliked the people that had lived inside It since Jerome Schwartz left and never came back (an abandonment and betrayal), the Apartment now confronted the fact: It couldn't put on the party without a tenant. The Apartment needed THEM. It needed guests. Zombie mimes, cowboys in drag, gangsters, the President and his First Lady, bald-headed Mr. Clean. It was pointless to have the party otherwise.

Unable to face it, the grim realization chased the Apartment--like one of Its own horror ill-illusions--back into the soft oblivion of dormancy.

It didn't even bother waking the next Halloween, the heart under the floorboards neither flopped or kicked.

It slept right through 9/11.

Five Halloweens passed by unnoticed, uncelebrated, ignored.

Then in December 2003, Roethke Sr. died of a brain aneurysm and the following year, his sons put Apartment #5 back on the market.

CHAPTER SIX:

SLEEPING WITCH

Martha Stuart's background is not essential in telling the history of Apartment #5. The Apartment didn't care about Martha's past, her life before she came to live in It--where she came from, who her parents were, why she dyed her hair black and bleached her skin pale, why she was addicted to snorting heroin. or the details of her crippling affair with her college professor and her college professor's wife--nothing mattered to the Apartment but that she was inside of It.

But as the one woman the Apartment loved (not that the Apartment "loved," it didn't, couldn't love, because the Apartment, being composed of only walls and floor and ceiling meeting in corners, was nothing but "surface" and could only love "surface" and what lay under the surface--the blood and bone and entrails, mucus and shit, bile and tears, sweat and inflamed tissue--the Apartment knew of, much of it had been spilled on Its floors, spattered on Its walls, seeped and caked into Its grains and creases like old meat caught between teeth, but it could not conceive of or credit either irony or pity, the crucial elements of love, as this story will describe), Martha Stuart should at least be sketched out more than to just say she was a poor little rich girl, lost and in exile, who found herself in the belly of a monster.

Born July 11, 1984, she grew up in Pasadena, California, but her parents "lived" in Hollywood. Her father, Levitt Stuart, was a film producer, up and coming. An only child, Levitt's parents died in a private-jet plane crash in Belize when he was away at boarding school. They were very wealthy (indeed it is only the very wealthy who can and do die in private-jet crashes) and he inherited enough money to keep him comfortable for the rest of his life. Her mother, Renee Belfont, was a pianist and composer born and Hungary, but raised in California since the age of nine. They met when she composed a score for a documentary he produced. They fell in love with what each could do for the other. She composed scores for two more of his film projects, the third was nominated for Academy Awards for best documentary and documentary musical score. They lost in both categories but by then they were married and she was already four months pregnant, and--worse--showing, on national television. No chance of an abortion now, though they had discussed it. She finally relented, provided it would be delivered via Caesarian section.

When their luck ran out in Hollywood, they refused to believe it was their fault, blaming instead the arrival of Martha Stuart. It was silently and secretly agreed upon between the two that keeping the baby had been a career move. Silently and secretly between them, but neither silent or secret when alone with Martha. Spooning cough medicine into her three-year-old daughter's mouth (the hacking was driving her nuts), Renee gently sang, "Mummy missed appearing at the Hollywood Bowl tonight because of you, darling. Opportunity doesn't knock twice. Rest, try to breath more shallowly." Levitt tucking her in, that broad smile he wore constantly like a rictus to hide his weak chin hovering over her, as he lilted, "Because of sweetie's diarrhea, Daddy is missing the biggest deal-making party of the Spring.

Yes, he is.   Now someone else is going to get Daddy's job.   Yes, they are."   Or the time her mother pulled up her blouse to show Martha her belly and the snake-shaped welt across it.   "See this scar. YOU gave mommy this scar."   Martha was only three and maybe they thought she couldn't understand, but Martha would always remember.   Tears imprint memories indelibly like that.

The truth of the matter was Levitt and Renee were not hurting financially, and they would not be hurting until the day they died (when they hurt a great deal). Even though they hadn't won their Oscars (registered trademark), the nomination on their resume of projects guaranteed they would always work in some capacity.   The problem was they, like most people, didn't want to work, they wanted to hit it big and then pick and choose their projects for the rest of their days.   Catered to and respected. Was that too much to ask?   This would never come true for them and they knew it in (what passed for) their hearts and they blamed Martha Stuart.   Things had been going great until she arrived, then their luck turned sour.

The sublime contempt they felt toward their daughter from the beginning might be encapsulated by the fact they named her Martha Stuart.   Levitt and Renee chose the name, not because it was associated with a relative, but because it sounded like Martha Stewart, and they thought that was a good thing.   They were basically unimaginative people.

Despite the different spelling, the name led to early taunting in school from dim-witted bullies.   It started the first day of the new school year in third grade.   Zoning had changed in the district where she lived and that year she attended a new school.

It was a school where the other children's parents were upwardly-mobile just like hers, but with a difference. For the most part her contemporaries had mothers and fathers who despite their faults, their appetites, their addictions, their indiscretions and their guiles, actually loved their sons and daughters and strived in life to make them feel happy and secure. For the most part, Martha Stuart's parents had learned to subcontract out the responsibilities of raising her to cleaning ladies and cooks, as well as therapists to handle the trickier bits. So in many ways, Martha Stuart was an alien among them. They sensed her difference, her otherness, and rejected her unconsciously, even before the teacher called the roll.

When Mrs. Armitage read her name from the S's on her sheet of new students, a titter of giggles and laughter spread across the classroom. It was just a matter of the other children recognizing the name from a boring TV show their parents always watched every Sunday. But then they all scanned the room looking for "Martha Stewart" and when Martha Stuart answered, "Here," the laughter redoubled. Martha Stuart did not look anything like Martha Stewart.

While both her parents were attractive, she had inherited their weaknesses and not their strengths: her father's diminutive chin and her mother's high forehead. Between these two landmarks: bettle brows, muddy green eyes, a snubnose like a kid's pressed up against a toy store window, and a slightly crenulated upper lip that looked like a krinkle-cut potato chip when she was on the verge of crying.

Her hair was mousey brown and stringy. Her shoulders sloped and no matter what clothes she wore they looked like a tube around her. That day she wore a skirt and her knees looked like axe-heads. She was drab and pudgy. The complete opposite of Martha Stewart.

Some kid shouted, "Hey, Martha Stewart, what you cooking today?"

The laughter was deafening, at least to Martha Stuart. What had she done?

The rest of the day, the kids giggled and pointed at her. Some girl taunted her about flower arrangements, Martha didn't even look up from her desk.

And that was only Day One of the rest of her life.

Nostalgia aids adults in forgetting that being in grade school is like being in prison, and you cannot escape contact with the other convicts. And if you are singled out for any reason, nothing will change it. Instead, you wake up every morning knowing someone is going to say something that will start them all laughing at you. On the bus. In the lunchroom. In the hallway on the way to the Lav. And this is only the THIRD grade. You see your life-sentence stretching out before you like the reflection of two opposing mirrors, day upon day upon day, unrelieved. This is what her parents had done to her naming her Martha Stuart. Without a backward glance. Whenever she thought of it, her upper lip turned into a potato chip.

Her existence went on like that with no detours for five years. Her summer vacations she spent dreading the return of school. It was all going to start again and there was nothing she could do about it. She explained this to her therapist in desperate sessions, but the advice she got was that she was making too much of it, creating her own demons.

Mostly she retreated into reading books. Classics, stories from a hundred years ago that had no mention of Martha Stewart. Poe, Dickens, Twain. It made her odd even among the other kids who read books, because they read new authors writing about what was happening NOW. She became a loner and loved herself about as much as her parents did.

She might have gone on like that until middle-age, except one afternoon she saw a movie called *Beetlejuice* on cable TV. It was the end of summer vacation before she entered the seventh grade. She'd never seen the movie before and actually tuned in halfway thru it, but as soon as Martha Stuart saw the character played by Winona Ryder, she was enthralled.

It happens that way when you are desperate for any avenue of relief, but when the character of Lydia said, "I'm unusual so I can see the unusual," she felt an instant kinship. It wasn't her fault she wasn't what everyone else wanted her to be. More than loving Winona Ryder, she wanted to be that character she was portraying, someone you would never call Martha Stewart.

She used black cardboard paint to color her hair the first time. It didn't work. Next time she used real hair dye. Her mother freaked out. It was the most emotion Renee had exhibited at her daughter since she was born. Martha needed no further encouragement.

The first day of seventh grade, when the homeroom teacher, Mr. Burke, called roll and said her name. She croaked out, "Mart-- It's Marty. Marty Stuart." A few of the kids laughed. Mr. Burke looked up, noted her appearance with a raised eyebrow, but corrected the roll call sheet, and dutifully called her Marty after that.

Her new appearance didn't win her any new friends, or stop the taunting, the same assholes she knew from the third grade continued to make the same tired jokes as if they were trapped in a web of their own stale imaginations. Except one kid in the lunchroom shouted at her, "Hey, Count Dracula, thought you only drank blood." It made his friends laugh as they walked away. And it made Marty smile, at least it was something different. When you're serving out your sentence, you take whatever you can get. Marty retreated behind her new look.

It was her misfortune that she never made that one friend or had that one teacher that can change a child's whole outlook. Her parents never even allowed her a pet, something to share her troubles with. Instead she slogged along alone as best she could. She graduated high school without ever having gone on a date. Not surprising that her first experience with a sexual relationship resulted in disaster and her turning to drugs.

It was in her first--and only--year in college. A love affair with her professor (in a course called The Social Construction of Reality) and with his wife, Mr. and Mrs. Noyes. Mr. and Mrs. No-Yes she came to think of them, because the odd passionate relationship--they were only a few years younger than her parents--only lasted two months before they sought to end it with her. But Marty was hooked, not only on the first loving relationship in her life but also on White Tiger.

Mrs. No-Yes was her introduction into snorting heroin. She'd had breast cancer five years previous, undergone chemotherapy and beat it. There had been a lot of pain and depression and her doctor prescribed an opioid for her to cope, but never unprescribed it as she got better. Mrs. No-Yes liked the way it made her feel and thru another of the professor's student liaisons had discovered something even better: heroin. After that she had a weekly-supply delivered, doses packed into square glassine envelopes, postage-stamp sized, rubber-stamped WHITE TIGER with the head of an oriental striped tiger printed on it.

One afternoon in bed, she shared some with Marty, and Marty reacted like hundreds of thousands of poor wretches before her: for the first time in her life she felt RIGHT in her skin. She was nothing. thought nothing, dreamt nothing. She felt erased and made free. She never wanted the sensation to end, but it was always only temporary, and yet more comfort than she had ever known in her life.

It was a bad combination. As Marty's need grew greater and she began showing up at their home unannounced and uninvited, Mr. and Mrs. No-Yes began to apply the brakes to their relationship. And Marty went through the windshield, figuratively and literally, dropping a cinderblock on the front of their cherry-red Miata parked in their driveway one Sunday morning when they refused to let her in. The police were called. Charges were not filed, her parents intervened. Neither they or the No-Yes-es wanted any of this to get in the press.

The following morning she poured paint thinner on the Hyundai rental in the No-Yes driveway and set it on fire. The police and fire departments were called. Charges were filed this time (no choice because it was a rental), and Marty was booked on three counts. But again, through the intervention of her parents (and a considerable outlay of money) the charges were dropped.

Levitt and Renee Stuart consulted their lawyer. They couldn't afford to have this going on. They considered having her committed to a rehab facility-- they clearly had a case to support it--but that seemed too temporary a solution, sooner or later she would be released and back in their lives. They wanted her gone for good. They'd seen other careers in Hollywood destroyed by kids-gone-wild, and they weren't going to let it happen to them.

They came up with a plan. She had two choices. Either they committed her to six months of rehab against her will or she moved away, as far away as they could imagine. New York City. Marty agreed to the second option and her parents had all the arrangements made through an apartment broker. They found her an apartment and paid to have it furnished. She left California forever with two suitcases, one of which held a zippered bag with 90 square glassine envelopes of White Tiger she had stolen from Mrs. No-Yes the month before things went to Hell. She had so many stashes stashed in reserve against a dwindling market, that she would never even know she'd been ripped off.

On June 11th, a month before her twenty-first birthday, Levitt and Renee Stuart shipped their daughter off to New York City. And in the months that followed, their lives got better. Impressive job offers began to flood in. The curse had been lifted. It was as if they were being rewarded for the actions. Or else just a coincidence, but they didn't think so.

***

The Apartment stirred, aware of movement inside it. First when a cleaning crew of two women entered it one sunny morning in late May, opened its windows, and cleaned its floor and surfaces. It didn't take long, but it was the first motion the Apartment had sensed inside It for five years, so Its attention was drawn. Next, furniture arrived, carried in by three men and arranged in a clump in the southwest corner of the Apartment. It was puffy over-stuffed furniture, all pastel pink and flower designed. The Apartment hated it, it was like have cotton crammed into Its mouth. After the movers left, no one came for another two weeks, and the Apartment lapsed back into dormancy, not curious about what was going to happen next, no idea Its life was about to change with the arrival of the new tenant.

***

The flight crew had trouble waking her when the airplane touched down in LaGuardia. She'd downed two packets of White Tiger at the start of the flight and hadn't so much as twitched through the whole journey. A couple of times one of the flight attendants leaned in close to make sure she was breathing. They'd had people o.d. on flights before, and the standard procedure was not to let the other passengers know. They finally got her to come round and standing on her feet. Once she was off the plane, she was airport security's problem.

But she came to. Somnambulistic ally she located her luggage, dragged them to the nearest exit, and waited in line until she caught a taxi into Manhattan, and then slept again--missing the skyline approach of her new home--not waking again until they arrived at the address printed on the tag on the set of keys her parents gave her. 65 Saint Marks Place #5.

Standing on a Manhattan sidewalk was nothing like she'd imagined. She'd always pictured skyscrapers and neon lights, people traveling in herds like cattle, jackhammers and police sirens. On the block she stood it was peaceful. Trees lined the sidewalk every twenty feet and some reached higher than the three- and four- story rowhouses they fronted. A heavy-set elderly woman walking a Chihuahua passed her without a glance. Marty heard sirens in the distance but they sounded faraway.

The enormity of the change in her life dropped on her like a piano. She was perspiring. Her buzz was wearing off, she needed to refuel. But that meant unpacking her bag, which meant going in to this strange brick-fronted building that looked ancient to her. She looked up at the windows and the zigzag of black fire-escape and wondered which was hers. Most of the windows had curtains and plants on their ledges, only the window to the left two stories above appeared completely blank.

A wide stoop of ten cement steps led up to the front entryway door. She brought her suitcases up one at a time. Tried two different keys before she found the one that turned in the lock. She walked inside and down the ground floor hallway, noting the door numbers. They only went as high as four. She lugged her suitcases up the stairs to the next landing, and then down the hall until she faced the scarred brown-painted metal door with "5" on it stenciled in gold paint.

Got the right key on the first try.

***

The Apartment slept on, undisturbed.

***

It wasn't what she expected and that made her happy, she'd imagined a sterile prison cell. Inside it was ten degrees cooler than the hallway and she felt the chill in the armpits of her damp shirt.

The apartment had old floorboards, an overpainted radiator, a white-enameled gas stove that was immediately to her left as she swung open the door. The apartment was the length and width of a tractor truck's semi-trailer. Half was taken up by the kitchen area with stove and twin-drained sink topped by a line of cabinets, open and empty. The further half ended into two uncurtained windows that glowed bright green from the tree branches directly outside. The left one opened onto the fire escape.

The bathroom was to her right past a window that opened to an air shaft. She hit the toilet first. A bathtub with shower attachment was compactly spaced beside the toilet. No shower curtain. The tiles soft pink. The built-in soap dish was black.

Next she went back to her suitcases, sat on the floor, and opened the one that held her stash (well, Mrs. No-Yes's stolen stash). It was inside a zippered yellow Hello Kitty bag.

She resisted the urge to count how many packets of White Tiger remained--it was early yet, there were plenty left--but she lost the battle and upended the bag on the floor and began counting them back into it. 86.

She tore open one of the packets, tapped out a thick worm of white powder between her left thumb and forefinger, lowered her head and inhaled it through her nose. 85.

Her anxiety abated. She explored the rest of the apartment. A rolled futon still packed in plastic wrap stood in one corner of the room. The rest of the room was taken up by the ugliest furniture she'd ever seen. Her mother must have personally picked it all out herself. Doughy, overstuffed armchairs upholstered in pastel pink and flower designs. She touched one and it gave off a perfumed potpourri scent.   The two chairs and matching loveseat and ottoman were like giant powder puffs.

She hated them and, as the first euphoric surge of the White Tiger hit her, Marty did something about it.

Propping the apartment door open with a suitcase, she slid all the furniture out into the hallway.   It was surprisingly light, or not surprisingly: both cheap and ugly.   All she left behind inside was a plain wooden kitchen table and the rolled futon.

Gravity helped her get it all down the stairs to the entryway hallway.   She kept expecting to encounter someone else living in the building, either coming in or going out and she rehearsed an apology in her head as she bounced the furniture between wall and banister, but everyone must've been out or in.

She took the ottoman outside first and carried it down the front stoop to the sidewalk.   Set it down beside a fire hydrant there, then thought better of it and moved it a few feet further down.   She didn't want a dog peeing on it.   Maybe somebody needed an ugly pastel pink ottoman.   It occurred to her that she should put a FREE sign on it, so people would know it was okay to take it.

She went upstairs, and by the time she'd found a green magic marker in her suitcase and a piece of notepaper to write the word FREE on and bring it back downstairs, the ottoman was gone.   She looked up and down the sidewalk to see if someone was carrying it away, but there was no one at either end of the block carrying anything.

She lugged down one of the armchairs and left the FREE sign on that instead.   When she came back with the second armchair, the first one was gone and so was the FREE sign.   She looked up and down the sidewalk again.   Again no one walking away with a chair.

That was quick work.   An old timey song her mother used to play in cabaret echoed in her head, "Like a New York minute."

Marty didn't bother making another sign.

She put out a small lacquered yellow endtable next, then sat for awhile on the steps of the front stoop, her front stoop, soaking up the sunshine.   A young Asian couple walked by dressed all in tea-colored leather.   They looked at the endtable, but kept going.

Marty went up the apartment to snort another line, she was starting to feel logy and didn't want to zone out before she'd finished the job, the loveseat was still blocking the downstairs hallway.   She emptied another packet of White Tiger on the web of flesh between forefinger and thumb--84--and went to the window that looked out on the vibrant tree, elm, she thought.

She   angled   and   looked   down   past   the sandstone ledge to the sidewalk two-stories below. The endtable was still there.

Getting the loveseat out the front entryway doorways provided a challenge.   Marty was wrestling with it, trying to get the angle right when a craggy voice called up to her,

"Moving out?"

Marty turned and looked down the stoop to the sidewalk and a white-haired old lady, tall and thin, wearing a white tanktop t-shirt and knee-length denim cut-offs, carrying two canvas totebags--one slung over each shoulder--full of groceries.

"No, actually, I'm moving in."

"Ahh," the old lady said.   "Know I haven't seen you before today.   Need some help?"

Before Marty could answer, the old lady had placed her canvas bags down on the endtable and was coming up the steps.   She wore smudged eyeglasses and through one of the lenses was a clear bright blue eye and through the other the eye had a gray filmy cast.   She smiled broadly.   Marty could see down her loose fitting t-shirt as she came up.   She only had one breast, the left one.

"I'm sure we can work it through," the old lady said, taking hold of one end.

"Uh, well..." Marty said.   "Actually I'm moving this *out*.   I...I...the apartment came pre-furnished and...it's not me."

The old lady cackled.   "I got you.   O.K. then, well, you stay where you are, just move that leg there and---"

The loveseat slipped easily out the door and together they carried it down to the sidewalk.

"Well, welcome to the neighborhood.   I'm Dori."

"I'm Marty," Marty said.

Dori picked up her canvas totebags from the endtable and slung them back over her shoulders. She looked at the endtable.

"I might come back for that when my hands aren't full.   If the Sidewalk Gods don't get it first.   I could use it in my living room."

"Sure, it's yours."   Marty laughed,   "But, you're right. Things have gone as fast as I put them out."

Dori nodded, grinning slyly. "The Sidewalk Gods," she said.   "Taking their offering. You'll see."

"What?   See what?"

"Well...next time you need something for your

129

new place, say.   You go out,   walk around the neighborhood, square a few blocks between here and 14th Street, you'll find what you are looking for.   The East Village is like that.   Call it coincidence, but the truth is: it's the Sidewalk Gods.   They give back. Swapsies."

Marty laughed.   She wasn't sure if this woman with the big toothy grin was being serious or not. Dori had a southern accent and it reminded her of old women in films who tell scary stories just to amuse you.   Marty was amused, but also weirded out.   Or else it was just the affect of the White Tiger, plus a heaping helping of jetlag.

"Radical," she said.   She'd never used that word before in her life.   She felt like she might throw up.

Dori looked up at the building.

"This where you're living?   I used to ball a guy who lived here back in the 80s.   Great bolero dancer. And the parties he threw on Halloween!"   She squinted up at the windows.   "Can't remember which one it was.   Well, Marty, I'll see you ar---"

Dori gasped and started to laugh. Marty had no idea why.

Dori pointed to the sidewalk behind her, pointing at nothing, a blank.   The ugly endtable was gone.

They both looked up and down the sidewalk but could see no one hefting it away.

"Huh, I guess..."   Marty wanted to say, "We just got distracted talking to each other, because you're the first person I've talked to in awhile, plus well, I'm sort of a drug addict," but she couldn't get it out, instead she just laughed with Dori and let her eyes go wide.

"Well, see you later, Marty." Dori trudged at a slightly bowlegged gait, her heavy canvas bags tilting her one way then the other, off in the direction of Second Avenue. Marty's eyes followed and her vision went telescopic. The next stage of White Tiger settling in, she could plop down right here on the front stoop and nod off and not move for hours, but that wasn't a good idea. Bad first impression.

She lingered long enough to take it all in. A church clock nearby chimed five o'clock. People were coming home from work. They seemed to be whizzing past her. All different shapes, colors, and attires, young and old. Some with canes, some on bikes. No one turned to notice her, standing--well, swaying--on her front stoop. Maybe it was the White Tiger coursing through her system, but she felt she was "home" and the sensation overwhelmed her, scared her. She felt happy.

She turned away and went back inside, had trouble with the keys, but finally made it.

Up in the apartment she tipped over the futon and unrolled it. Flopped down on it without taking off the plastic. She stared up at the ceiling. It was cracked and repaired. At its center was a ceiling fixture fitting in plaster relief, decorated in Grecian laurels, and comprised of three bare unlit lightbulbs, that at this angle stared down on her like a moued clownface.

She wished she had more furniture to offer to the Sidewalk Gods. She closed her eyes then drifted into purring nothingness of White Tiger, her head using the Hello Kitty bag as a pillow.

Such a newbie in New York City, she'd forgotten to lock the apartment door behind her, and it remained unbolted the whole time she slept in her torpid oblivion.   But she was safe.   None of the other tenants who passed the door would ever have thought of going into #5.

***

The   Apartment   slept   on,   slightly   more peacefully with the extraction of the puffy furniture, but still not awake. Yet.

***

Marty woke nine hours later, not having moved so much as a millimeter.   White Tiger was like that: when it pounced, it paralyzed you.

She came to from a dream.   Mrs. No-Yes had discovered her stash was gone and knew Marty stole it.   She came at Marty vengefully with a hat pin. Marty woke up.   No idea where she was, but that her bladder was stabbing her like a hat pin.   She recombobulated enough to remember where the bathroom was and struck out for it on hands-and-knees finally evolving into an upright stagger by the time she reached the bathroom door.   She landed herself on the toilet seat and pissed for 47 seconds.

Dreaming of Mrs. No-Yes depressed her, because she realized she didn't miss her or Mr. No-Yes.   Had she ever loved them?   Or was her obsession driven more by her love of the White Tiger? Her screaming that she loved them and they had to let her in was as much about getting to Mrs. No-Yes's stash and not about getting into bed with them. That had just become a means to an end.

And her initial attraction to them, giving into their seduction wasn't that just a transparent transference, a kinky surrogate father and mother? It depressed her even more her psyche was so trite and obvious, yet beyond her control to alter.

She didn't miss Mr. and Mrs. No-Yes, but strangely she missed her parents, even though they rarely interacted. Her father would be in his study blasting 80s techno music. Her mother in the kitchen concocting the slimy green kale gruel which was part of her newest diet, filling the house with its noxious fumes. While Marty lay on her bed and read. It was a routine she was used to, and she missed it.

Back on the futon, she unzipped the Hello Kitty bag for a packet of White Tiger and used it. 83. The thought chilled her. She did the math. How long could it last, how long could she MAKE it last? And then what? Quit? She unzipped the bag again and got another packet. 82.

It made her feel better, even though she knew she just made the situation worse. She rode yesterday's high into this morning's and fell back to nothingness.

Five hours later, dehydration roused her again, with a cotton mouth and a headache starting in her temple and threading to a point behind her right eye.

She did the crawling on all fours gag again and climbed up to the white basin of the kitchen sink. She let the water run until it was good and cold, and also because the first spurt that came out of the faucet was brown with rust as if it hadn't been turned on for years.

The water helped the cotton-mouth and splashing her face partly relieved the pain in her temple, but she needed coffee, caffeine, to really relieve it.

She grabbed her keys, credit card, and sunglasses and headed out the door, having trouble unlocking it until she realized it wasn't locked at all. She shook her head at herself and stumbled down the hall.

On the sidewalk in front of her building was a chair, not one of hers, a wicker chair with a hole punched in the seat. Not a good offering, she mused, remembering yesterday, like it was a pleasant dream she had.

A spiky-haired woman with nose, eyebrow, ear, and lip piercings walked by sipping from an orange cardboard cup. Marty headed in the direction she'd come from the corner of St. Mark's Place and First Avenue. She gazed around the intersection, no immediate prospects for coffee except for the bodega across the street, they had to have coffee. But she turned left in search of a real coffeeshop and around the corner, between a greasy municipal metal-wastebasket and a heavily tagged and scratched telephone booth kiosk was a giant white hand. It was three feet high and sat on the end of its wrist, a molded plastic sculpture of a cupped hand reaching upward with long, tapered fingernails. It was a few second before it hit her:

It wasn't a sculpture, it was a chair!

Without even thinking, Marty sat down on it. It was *just right*. She smiled, a phrase from a fairy tale.

She stood up, looked at its base. It wasn't bolted down. She tilted it by the fingernail tip of its forefinger--it was a left hand--and it put up no resistance, it was so light. Had to be hollow.

She lifted it by the thumb and looked all around her. She didn't put it down again until she was back at her building digging in her pocket for her keys. All the way back she expected to hear pursuing feet and shouts of "Hey, that's mine!" but they never came. Instead, in her head, she heard Dori telling her, "They give back. Swapsies."

She placed the chair by the window in her apartment that looked out on the leafy elm tree. It caught a mottled slant of late afternoon sun in its palm. For something she'd got off the sidewalk, it was clean, white as a baby's first tooth. Her first piece of furniture that was hers. She sat in it, wondering if there was a mate. A right hand out there, up-stretched, on a further block's corner. The idea made her get up again--or else she could've sat in the hand all day--to go out and look for its opposite. And get the coffee she'd set out for to begin with.

She didn't go back to First Avenue, instead turned right this time toward Second, passing mainly other residential apartment houses, but across the street was a ground-level Sushi bar advertising crocodile on its sandwich board. Crocodile? Did people really eat--

She almost walked right into it. A floor lamp standing out on the curb. She faced a stained-glass lamp shade on a black wrought iron rod and base. The stained glass was alternating strips of red and white and bowed so that the shade looked like a circus tent, and even a tiny metal flag painted red topped its frame. But more than that, hanging from the eight corners of the shade, were eight evenly-spaced black bats sculpted in glass.

Marty laughed. It reminded her of that scene at the end of *Beetlejuice*, when Michael Keaton's head turns into a carousel. She stepped away from it, she didn't dare touch it, it looked expensive. There was *no way* someone just left this out on the sidewalk.

A piece of paper was pinned down by one of the four wrought-iron clawed feet that made the base of the lamp. The word FREE printed on it in green magic marker.

She lifted up the lamp with both hands. It was heavy, but she didn't have far to carry it. She tried to pick up the FREE sign (just to throw it away, not litter), but it was stuck to the ground by a gooey wad of red gum, so leaving it was better than someone stepping in that.

But it weirded her out. It looked a lot like the sign she made, even though it was just four block letters. Everyone made block capitals the same way. And if it was the same sign, her sign, did someone place it there for her? Was someone watching her? Even now as she carried the lamp back to her apartment? Was it just paranoia or a possibility?

The thing was, she didn't consider it a possibility. She'd only been in Manhattan a day, that would be pretty quick work for a stalker. It was the other possibility that both bothered and intrigued her. "Swapsies."

That was crazy. But it didn't stop her from going right back out again as soon as she'd dropped off the floor lamp.

This time Marty crossed to the opposite side of the street, didn't pass anything interesting, but did find a coffeeshop at the corner of Second Avenue and bought a cup there, hot and sweet, from a balding young man with a moustache like Salvador Dali.

She strolled south down Second Avenue, past an off-Broadway theater called The Orpheum, restaurants--Indian, Chinese, Vietnamese, Greek, Ukrainian--to the next sidestreet and turned left on East Seventh Street.

And it was crazy, but halfway down the block there was a tall, narrow armoire in wine-dark finish, and from a distance it looked shaped exactly like an up-ended casket, the hinges protruding like pall-bearer handles.

As she approached, two people, a man and a woman both heavily tattooed, both pony-tailed, in their late thirties, were examining it, discussing it. The man put his arms around it and lifted it, and put it back down, shaking his head, whether because it was too heavy or too light, she couldn't tell, but the couple walked away from it, holding hands covered in ink and thick silver rings.

Marty approached the armoire. She loved it, even before she placed her hand against the smooth veneer of the door and the pressure sprung a catch and the lid--the door--swung open. The interior was lined in vermillion satin. A mahogany top rod suspended two wooden hangers that swung languidly to and fro.

Marty loved it. She wanted to crawl inside it and shut the door behind her. Maybe disappear, or better yet reappear. She wanted it, but she'd need a handtruck to get it back to her building. Experimentally, she hugged it like the tattooed man had done and lifted it up to get a feel for its weight. She almost fell back over. Had to adjust her footing. It was so light, like it was made of balsa wood. Maybe it was, maybe it was just some theater prop, probably why the man and woman left it behind, not serviceable enough. But it suited Marty perfectly.

Leaving her half-drunk coffee forgotten on the sidewalk, she carried her new find back to her apartment. She hardly broke a sweat.

She almost stopped for a toot of White Tiger. She hadn't had any since she got up and it growled to be taken. But she was on a roll, she felt it, and riding a different high, she wanted more.

She found it out on the corner of East Fifth Street and First Avenue, across from a McDonald's.

An ornate, mirrored vanity dresser so ugly it was beautiful. It was old and stunk of a basement and festooned all around the mirror were sturdy dust-furry cobwebs. It was Mrs. Haversham's desiccated wedding cake turned into a piece of furniture.

No longer wondering why, Marty knew it was there for her. Like she was being welcomed.

But getting this piece home--she was thinking of the apartment as home now--was going to be tricky, despite the fact it was on castors. But she loved the fact that, with all things she'd been carting back, no one stopped to look at her strangely along the way, no one seemed to even notice what she was doing. Marty adored this most of all. Her entire life she'd been singled-out as odd, but now she was passing people who made her look plain and ordinary by comparison. The anonymity was like cool stream water.

She carefully rolled the vanity dresser the three blocks back to her front stoop--the casters held up--then considered her options. First she took the drawers out--seven of them, three on each side, one in the center--and carried them up to the apartment. Next she examined the back. The mirror was detachable. She detached it. It was heavy, the heaviest part. She carried it carefully trying not to disturb a single thread of the accumulated spiderwebs.

The remaining empty dresser she got upstairs one step at a time.

She reconstructed it beside where her futon lay.

Again she didn't stop for a line of White Tiger, but went back out. She was having too much fun "shopping."

By seven P.M. she had refurnished her whole apartment and she was hungry.

She went to the Chinese restaurant on Second Avenue and got Low Mein, Chow Mein, Egg Rolls, Fried Rice and Wonton Soup. She picked at it on the apartment floor, just a bite of the egg roll and gulps of the soup. The rest she put in the refrigerator. Except the refrigerator, while clean and empty, was also warm inside. She set the bag of take-out inside it, found its cord and a wall socket, and plugged it in.

For dessert, she snorted her first line of White Tiger since breakfast. 81. It pounced on her fast. She sank into nothingness, surrounded, guarded, protected by her furniture: the casket armoire, the wedding-cake vanity, the circus tent lamp, and the giant white hand armchair.

***

About then the Apartment woke up.

It thought It had overslept. Dormant so long and vacant to boot, It no longer registered time, but something different triggered Its odd chronometer. Gradually, reluctantly, even truculently, It became aware again. What was it? Autumn already? No. The trees outside Its windows full of vibrant green leaves.

But inside It, somehow, some way, it was...incomprehensibly Halloween.

The Apartment had slept through New York City's most catastrophic terrorist attack, barely registering the seismic shock of the Twin Towers collapsing into rubble and dust a mile away, but the mere hint of Halloween roused and aroused It from slumber like a clanging bell.

It didn't believe Its senses.

But what other conclusion could It draw?

The wads of suffocating pink furniture It last recalled were gone.   In its place:

A coffin!

Bats on a carousel!

A giant white hand!

Spread out on a plastic-wrapped bed, a giant black witch ragdoll!

A vanity mirror dresser decorated in spiderwebs.

The Apartment was baffled.

And then the black witch stirred on the mattress.

It spooked the Apartment.   A new experience. It wasn't used to being on the receiving end of fright.

Some sort of battery-operated thing like the silent rubber heart which lay bedded under Its floorboards below the mattress.   Very realistic.   The witch made no other sound or motion for a long time after that, its batteries evidently low.   But then suddenly--well, six and a half hours later--the witch awoke!   Rolled off the mattress onto Its floor, crawled, then walked to the bathroom where it peed in Its toilet.

It dawned on the Apartment: This isn't a Halloween prop, this is the new tenant.   My new tenant.

Returning from the bathroom, the witch drank water directly from Its kitchen faucet.   Its cabinets were empty of glasses, cups, and brick-a-brack.

She went back to the mattress and flopped down on it.   From a bag on the floor she took a smaller bag, ripped it open, and poured out white powder--like plaster dust--onto her hand.   She lowered her head and the dust disappeared.

She collapsed back on the mattress and didn't stir for seven hours, completely inert and soundless.

Her shadow moved more than she did as the angle of sunlight changed throughout the day. The Apartment Itself moved more and made more noise, the heat of the season swelling joists and joints, making It pop and creak

She was unlike any tenant It had known. No commotion. The Apartment was fascinated. And even though it was obviously still Summer--far from Autumn--It didn't retreat back to dormancy but stayed awake and watched the new tenant sleep, focusing Its dull attention on her like the rays of a never-waning full moon.

She was both the Witch and Sleeping Beauty. Sleeping Witch. In her static state she was as immobile as the Apartment. Her breath so soft, the Apartment had to strain every grain and fiber of wood to sense it through Its floorboards. The Apartment was in commune with the tenant. Its love started as a sense of kinship.

And at least in this, the Apartment was close to being right. A shared experience of separation and neglect, abandonment of a unit. Marty was another amputated limb, standing independent of a body.

At one point that afternoon, a blue-bottle fly buzzed in through a crack in Its window frame and after a barnstormer's tour of the surroundings, honed in on the sleeping woman and settled unceremoniously upon her face.

Where it crawled for twenty-one minutes, concentrating on her nose and mouth, but also tasting and puking from her eyes and ears. For all the reaction she had--not even an involuntary twitch-- the woman might as well have been dead.

When the fly got bored with that, it took another whirligig tour of the Apartment, finally settling for a rest on the surface of one of the white walls.

And the Apartment slurped it in in mid Zzz--

Sleeping Witch slept on, unviolated, for two more hours, well into night.

And when she did finally wake, it was sudden and dramatic.

She woke up screaming.

***

One of the drawbacks of opioid abuse, of substances such as White Tiger, is that the consumption of them leads to severe digestive complications. Painful complications, such as constipation of the worse variety. The body cannot properly process these foreign substances and they calcimate and harden in the system resulting in back-ups. The addict's inactivity doesn't help. The results are a combination of hemorrhoids and feces sharp as rough-hewn coal shards, and the desperate need to void them.

Not that this impeded her use of White Tiger, instead increased it to combat the pain. In one hour after waking, she consumed three packets. 78.

It didn't help, instead it sent her to the bathroom to spend the rest of the next day, a Saturday, sitting on the toilet, straining to pass something, crying and groaning into a towel she pressed into her mouth.

Stabbed from within, but too wigged-out and in agony to do anything but muffle her screams to her ears and the echoing bathroom tile walls around her. The only thought in her head now: I'm never going to do White Tiger again, I'm never going to do White Tiger again, I'm going to flush all the rest of it down the drain and never do White Tiger again.

Finally, she passed something black as coagulated blood and the shape and size of a scaly iguana. It was immediately followed by a massive release of pent-up gas, which had caused her as much pain as the passing of the spiky turd.

Her legs were too shaky to stand. She curled up on the bathroom's tiled floor with the towel (full of her agonized groans) as a pillow. And slept.

***

The Apartment was powerless to help. All It could do was watch her suffer, and then sleep, bunched up on Its cold tile floor.

***

About three hours later, Marty regained consciousness.

She got to her feet and followed her established path from bathroom, to kitchen faucet, to mattress, to Hello Kitty bag. She snorted half a packet of White Tiger and went back to sleep with the half-empty packet in her fist. 76 & 1/2.

***

She slept again and the Apartment relaxed. It explored the new Haunted House exhibits. The casket, the carousel, the hand. The hand! The Apartment reached for it.

The Apartment tried to flex it.

It was immobile.

It was heavy.

So was the casket.

Maybe it was because they were new.

***

Marty awoke feeling much better. Overdoses that a person survives often result in feelings of euphoria once they have passed.

She stretched and sighed and opened her eyes.

The clownface ceiling fixture OOoo-ed down at her with its two lightbulb eyes and lightbulb mouth.

"Good morning," she said to the ceiling.

***

The Apartment heard.   Did she...speak to It?

***

Marty still felt shitty, but she needed to get coffee.   Something to put in her stomach—other than the rest of the half packet of White Tiger--that wouldn't turn into a terror in her entrails.   A donut. A plain donut.

She changed her clothes from her still-unpacked suitcase.   From a black lace pull-over and black knee-length skirt she changed into a black t-shirt and black jeans.

She closed her suitcase and then opened it again.   Began unpacking, filling her new casket armoire with all her belongings, but not filling it at all, still plenty room left inside it.

She took the empty suitcase to the apartment's one closet and pushed it in.

Overhead, something shifted, on a shelf above the clothing-rack rod.   A cardboard box.   And more stacked up above and behind it. Huh?   She'd have to check that out. After coffee.

She left the apartment to explore more of her new neighborhood.

***

The Apartment missed her.   Awaited her return.

***

Marty was surprised to find it was Sunday. Late in the afternoon.   Plenty of people were out. She wandered, getting a sense of her surroundings. Two blocks east was a city park, Tompkins Square. She walked its curving paths, past jungle gyms, a handball court, and finally sitting on a bench by the dog run, and watching the owners and dogs interact.

Walking back, she found a used bookshop and after an hour left with a purchase of a hardcover copy of Samuel Richardson's *Clarissa*, one thousand five hundred and thirty-four pages of 18th-century English literature, thick as an unabridged dictionary, and for only $8.99.

And then she saw Dori, waiting for the light to change at First Ave. and East 7th Street, again with full canvas totebags hung over each shoulder.

The first thing Dori said was, "You need feeding up."

Marty laughed. "I came out for a something to eat and got distracted looking around."

She held up *Clarissa*.

She blathered on. She could feel herself doing it, but couldn't help herself, it had been so long since she'd talked to anyone.

"Oh, and I didn't tell you! I have to tell you. The Sidewalk Gods, you were right."

And she told Dori all about what happened, and now she felt like the crazy one saying it all and believing it.

The whole time Dori stood there listening and laughing with her canvas totebags slung on her shoulders, each holding twenty pound bags of potting soil she'd picked up from the 7th St. hardware store. Marty started to feel bad.

"I'm sorry, I'm holding you up."

"No, just on my way home."

"Well, I'll see--"

"Actually," Dori said, and groaned a little, massaging the small of her back, "maybe you could help me carry these back. I only live a few blocks away. Twelfth and Second Ave."

"Sure," Marty said.

"You'll have to take both of them," Dori said. "I can carry both, but I can't carry one. Balance."

"Sure," Marty said again.

She added *Clarissa* to one of the canvas totebags and slung both bags over one shoulder, but after about a block of walking and chatting with Dori, she slung one over each shoulder, it was the better way. Dori made no comment, but kept talking and pointing out the best shops to check out. "That place makes the best desserts, Veneiro's, check it out when you need a treat." "If you ever need shoes repaired, just there is this little Jewish man who will re-sole and make them better than what you bought."

As they turned the corner of East Eleventh Street and Second Avenue, they came upon a small cluster of four people, standing and looking down at the sidewalk. Nearer she got, Marty saw what they were looking at: a pigeon, flopping around on the sidewalk, clearly injured.

The on-lookers—all dressed in nice evening sportswear—were commiserating and trying to decide what to do. "The poor thing must have been hit by a cab or something." "We should find a box." "Who should we call?"

As Dori approached, she stopped, looked down, and then squatted to the sidewalk. She picked up the thrashing pigeon between her thin wrinkled hands, cupped its head in her right hand and twisted. The pigeon went instantly still.

Dori walked off, carrying it.

The on-lookers were speechless. Their jaws hung slack. They did not blink.

Marty ran with her burden to catch up with Dori who was dropping the dead pigeon into the nearest city wastebasket.

Breathless, Marty said, "I've never seen anything like that."

Dori cackled.

"I grew up on a farm in Florida. That's how we killed the chickens before we plucked 'em. That was the easy part, plucking tears up your hands. This is my place here."

She lived in a building that adjoined an old off-Broadway Theatre that used to put on Yiddish plays. Dori lived three stories up in the roof apartment. The wide open space was mainly taken up by two long sofas opposite a coffeetable covered in magazines and facing a wide-screen TV. A dining table set with four placemats was otherwise cluttered to overflowing by a sewing kit, stacks of cut out coupons, postcards, pens, and a hundred other things. And all four walls were lined with bookshelves, crowded with books.

Marty entered it and deposited the canvas bags of potting soil on the carpeted floor. She felt like a Sherpa.

She rolled her eyes, marveling at Dori. "I can't believe you climb all those stairs with these heavy bags."

"Like I said, grew up on a farm, you get used to hauling loads. But I've been living here in New York City since 1957. Here, sit down, I'll get us a glass of wine. You like eggplant parmigiana?"

Marty had never liked eggplant parmigiana until that night.

Dori poured out her history along with red wine to Marty and they ate eggplant parmigiana together. At first, Marty had trouble not staring at Dori's filmy gray eye—it was like the Master's eye in Poe's The Tell-Tale Heart--or at the empty spot in the front of her t-shirt where one of her breasts no longer was, but gradually it didn't matter anymore. Anymore than how Marty herself looked.

Dori grew up in Florida, a small parish outside of Dayton. She was the youngest of four children, three older brothers, the youngest five years her senior. They grew up on a farm, mainly chickens and goats, and an acre of tomatoes, carrots, cucumbers, and corn, and two apple trees. She and her family lived off the land. She grew up a tomboy, climbing trees and catching frogs.

Her older brothers all married young and spawned sons and daughters. Dori became the permanent nanny and babysitter that the brothers dumped their brood on, because she was unattractive and strange and would probably never get married and have children of her own. They were right about the last part, but wrong about Dori putting up with it. When she turned eighteen, she fled the life of servitude. She packed a single suitcase and left on a bus for New York City without ever saying goodbye. For years, her family thought she'd been abducted and killed, though they never got around to reporting her disappearance to the police. They weren't *that* concerned, more "put out" that they now had to raise their children on their own.

She didn't know a single person in New York City when she moved here. She checked into the YWCA, left her suitcase unopened, and struck out to pound the pavement looking for a job.

Back home, she had got a reputation for floral arrangements and had been exploited at all three of her brothers' wedding and at those of several cousins to create the table centerpieces free of charge. She developed a talent for it, and so she stopped at every florist she passed as she weaved her way up and down the avenues of Manhattan, feeling every inch of the country bumpkin that she was. She finally came across a sidestreet below Penn Station that seemed to be ALL plants, with trucks delivering and picking up.

She walked into a place called Michaelson's and overheard a phone conversation of the man behind the counter, explaining how there was no way he could produce the 24 Orchid corsages by the weekend. It was impossible.

Dori stepped up to the counter and told the man she could do it by ten o'clock tomorrow morning.

The clerk—who turned out to be the owner, Michaelson—told her she was crazy. He laughed in her face, "I don't even have 24 Orchids, lady."

"What if I do it?" Dori challenged him. She had stopped in a small florist on E 81st two hours before and knew where she could get the orchids.

"Hang on a sec," Michaelson said into the phone, then pressed the receiver to his chest. "So, you're asking me a price? You need money?"

"I need a job."

Michaelson raised his eyebrows. Shrugged.

"You're on, lady," he said, then back to the phone receiver. "Listen, lunchtime tomorrow. I'll see what I can do. But it'll be extra. Fine. Goodbye."

They introduced themselves, agreed terms, and Dori walked out of the shop straight back to the florist on E. 81st, got there right before the shop closed. The little old lady who ran the place took pity on her and gave her a bargain, recognizing a desperation in her face that reminded her of her own youth in Yugoslavia.

She stayed up all night in her room at the YWCA, but had finished the job well before dawn. It was so easy, maybe because she was doing the work for herself for a change. But if this is what passed for fast work in New York City, she just might have a chance here.

And she did. That first job blossomed into a forty-year career as a floral arranger and designer. She rose to the position of floral arranger for all the ceremonial events at the Lincoln Center, until a diagnosis of breast cancer put an end to her career, but not her life. Following a mastectomy and the remission of her cancer, she retired on her investments and the amazing $200 a month rent she paid for her rooftop space. Occasionally she still did a job or two as a favor.

"Then what's all the potting soil for?" Marty asked.

Dori showed her her roof garden. It was dark by then, but Dori switched on some floodlamps. It was a flat aluminum-plated New York City rooftop, but upon it in rows were fifty or sixty buckets and containers full of growing plants. Sunflowers. Tomatoes. Cucumbers. Blueberry and raspberry bushes. Rhubarb. Eggplant. Lilies. Pansies. Radishes. Four four-foot high beanstalks.

And all around them in the night air, the sounds of New York City. Sirens. Car horns. Laughter. Music. And the skyline! From Dori's roof Marty could see the spires of the Empire State Building and the Chrysler Building, lit up like rocketships awaiting countdown. They were the first authentic sites of New York she had seen since moving here. Marty couldn't believe this, a vast flower and vegetable garden existing in this metropolis.

It made her yearn for a snort of White Tiger. She wanted to disappear into this garden. But she also needed some White Tiger, it was growling.

Marty said, "I should get going."

"I have strawberry shortcake for dessert."

Marty stayed.

They watched *60 Minutes* on TV, each sprawled out on one of the couches, and were both fast asleep after 41 minutes.

***

As it grew dark, the Apartment got worried. Where was she? Was she okay? It knew people sometimes did not come back when they left, like Jerome did, but she only just got here, she only just moved in. Where was she?

***

Marty woke the next morning at eight A.M. The opposite couch was empty. The whole room was empty, even the bathroom, which Marty used right away. Finally, she followed the hallway to the door onto the roof.

Dori was outside in her cut-off shorts and sweaty t-shirt, lugging plastic gallon jugs of water she filled from a garden hose along the far brick wall to all the various plants lining the granite parapet of the roof.

"Good morning!" Marty said.

Dori pulled earplugs-- linked to walkman radio clipped to the front of her cut-offs—from her ears and said good morning back. "Got to water them early, before the sun gets too high."

"Let me help."

"Grab a jug. Or fill a jug."

They spent all of Monday morning tending to the garden. After coffee, Marty begged off. It wasn't just the growls calling her back to the White Tiger, that wasn't so bad, but she felt if she stayed her now with Dori a moment longer, she would never want to leave.

"Thanks for your help, Marty."

"See ya, Dori." And she left.

But all the way back to her place, Marty thought, wow, so this is what it's like to have a pal, huh? And it didn't seem to matter that Dori was over 50 years her senior; Dori was like a little kid, an eternal kid. She was Tom Sawyer. The notion made Marty smile.

Dori had explained to her during the night. "I learned early on if I was going to have a continuing social life in New York City, I'd have to keep meeting younger people who moved here, because all the friends I made when I first moved here, got married, had kids, moved to the suburbs, grew up. So I realized, if I was going to be a lifer, I'd have to make a new crop of friends every decade or so."

Marty smiled all the way home. Her parents had sent her here as a punishment, but unwittingly, they'd delivered her home. It was almost like a fairy tale, only without the dragon.

When she got home, she couldn't open her door. The streetdoor was fine, but when she got up to the apartment door, it wouldn't unlock. She tried all the keys on her ring, none of them worked. She knew by now which key it was, but it stubbornly wouldn't turn the deadbolt and unlock the door. She stood there frustrated for five minutes, embarrassed that she may have to go back to Dori's and ask her for help. Find a locksmith.

The deadbolt clicked, like a revolver cocking. The scarred metal door of #5 drifted in of its own weight.

Marty stood on the threshold.   The apartment was pitch dark.

It was as if someone was on the other side and Marty held her breath, standing her ground, feeling safer in the well-lit hallway, able to run away if she had to.

Nothing happened.

She waited a long time, long enough for people to arrive.   Someone buzzed an apartment above her and in turn were buzzed in.   The downstairs door opened and male and female voices echoed up the stairwell.

As the couple reached her landing, Marty reached her hand in and found the light switch just inside the door and turned it on as she pushed open the door.

No one on the other side of the door.   The couple passed behind her, continuing up to the next landing.

Marty walked in.

Checked the bathroom. No one. The rest of the apartment was visible to her, no place to hide, except that closet.

The closet was open and half outside its door was a jumbled pile of brown cardboard boxes.   The boxes from the upper shelf.   One must've fallen and the rest avalanched out (she reasoned).

She leaned over one of the boxes--its flap was open--and inside she saw...

Hands!

Forgetting her trepidation, Marty sat on the floor and started unpacking.   It was like Christmas for her.   She got her Hello Kitty bag, ripped open a packet of White Tiger—75—and rode the essential high as she put up all the discovered decorations.
***

The Apartment had just been sulking.   But with her laughing and putting everything up now, the

Apartment couldn't help but forgive her for staying out all night, carousing.

***

July and August were a happy honeymoon time for all parties concerned. Marty helped every other day at Dori's garden or with the shopping, she was building up muscle mass again. One day, Dori told her, "Marty, I appreciate all your help, but I feel like I'm keeping you from your own work."

Marty confessed she had no work, confessed more, confessed everything. Told her everything about her parents, about the No-Yeses, about her use of White Tiger. The last bit of news, Dori took gravely.

"Never liked junkies," she stated, "I've known too many of them."

"I'm just using it until it's all gone," Marty said, and even to her ears it sounded phony, because the days she wasn't with Dori, she spent zonked out on White Tiger, reading Clarissa until she fell once again into stupor.

This kept the Apartment content, despite Marty's overnight absences (becoming more frequent) from which she returned smelling of fertilizer. The Apartment had come to accept this. As long as she eventually returned home to It, the Apartment was satisfied.

The Apartment liked best when she was high on the white powder and just lay there silently, Its Sleeping Witch. Sometimes she roused half-awake and touched herself and made herself moan and the Apartment felt her quivering vibrating through Its floorboards.

The new tenant named the Apartment one day. As she was leaving one morning to get her cup of coffee, she turned and said aloud, "Be back in a bit, Five."

Five.   It was Five.

***

Things went along well until trouble started in early September.   Marty's parents came for a surprise visit.

Levitt and Renee Stuart had been invited to attend a 9/11 memorial ceremony at the Met.   The other names on the guest list persuaded them to accept the invitation and make the trip from their beloved West Coast to Manhattan.

And--kill two birds--they could check up on Martha Stuart and see what she was up to.

They didn't call or e-mail to announce their visit.   They wanted it to be a surprise.   They had their own set of keys provided by the broker.

And it was fortunate, too (or unfortunate, depending on your outlook) that they did arrive at her apartment with keys, because that afternoon Marty was drifting deep on a White Tiger ride and didn't respond when they buzzed, or knocked once they let themselves in the building.   So they used their key to enter the apartment.

***

The Apartment tensed.   Every board creaked like someone cracking their knuckles.   Its door was opening.   People were coming in.   The tenant was asleep.   Don't wake the tenant.   DON'T WAKE HER.

***

"What in the hell..." her father said, taking in all the decorations.

"Where's all the furniture I bought?" her mother said.

They walked in.   The door swung shut behind them.   Softly.

"Martha!" her father said.

They found her on her futon mattress on the floor.   She'd never gotten around to taking off the plastic.   The Hello Kitty bag was unzipped at her side and the remaining bags of White Tiger had spilled out.

"Martha!" her mother said.

Marty didn't stir.   Her breathing was just to be assumed.

"I don't believe it," Levitt said. "No, I do believe it."

"Where's the furniture I bought?" Renee asked again, to the apartment in general.

"Well, this is the last straw," Levitt said.

"I bet she sold it for drugs," Renee said.

"We can't let this go on.   She needs to learn. Maybe if she faces being homeless it will inspire her to get her life together.   We need to cut ties."

Renee said nothing, still brooding over the missing furniture, but her silence was their mutual agreement.

"Get up, Martha," Levitt said, and nudged her foot with the toe of his shoe.

A loud KICK-FLOP erupted from below the futon, it moved their daughter's foot.

They jumped back.

A loud KNOCK, like crunched timber, erupted from behind them.

"Hello?" Levitt said, moving toward the apartment door, trailed by his wife.   No answer. "Hello?"   He reached for the knob of the door and turned.   It wouldn't turn.

KNOCK!

He sprang back, colliding with his wife.

There was a peephole.   Levitt leaned forward and placed his eye against it.

Squinting and focusing, he saw nothing but empty hallway.

KNOCK!

He jumped and jabbed the peephole in his eye.

"Fuck," he said. "Shit."

"Levitt, that came from over here." She pointed toward the open closet door. "Is it the pipes?"

Renee wandered over to the closet.

Levitt said, "My fucking eye. Where's the bathroom?" Through wobbly tears, he spied pink bathroom tiles through an open door and headed for it as his wife stepped into the empty closet.

"It's empty," Renee said, and the door shut behind her.

In the bathroom, Levitt couldn't find a sink, only a bathtub faucet. He leaned in and started the water running, splashing it onto his sore eye. He dried his face with the bathroom's only towel. Experimented looking through his sore eye at himself in the medicine cabinet mirror. Blurred, but otherwise okay. He splashed more water on.

The water wasn't going down the drain. It was clogged. Black hair and green gunk. His daughter was disgusting, not to—

It moved. The black hair and gunk moved. It was a rat!

He shrank back an inch, stopped.

No, just black hair and gunk, shimmering under the running water. He leaned over and closing his bad eye, looked down at it with his good eye.

The gunk was BIGGER than before it, it was...

Unreal, like something in a movie Levitt thought as it

SPRANG up and fastened on his face, yanked him down with a ker-splash into the half full tub, now more than half full with him drowning inside it.

The gunk held him fast as he thrashed, as bubbles burst out, until both dwindled to silence and stillness.

***

The Apartment didn't want to wake her. It had to maneuver, use finesse. The unavoidable yips of terror would pass unnoticed like an ambulance siren out on the street, but It had to limit the screams or risk waking her.

Once the woman was in the closet, she was neatly subsumed, into the Apartment's walls like lotion on skin. Her hands were the last things to go. They were so beautiful, so structured, the Apartment wanted to keep them or casts of them.

The man took more time to get down the drain, but it was done before she woke again.

***

Marty came to from a dream of her mother, it seemed so real she could almost smell the lingering scent of her favorite perfume.

She went and peed in the bathroom, then went back to bed, and after another toot of White Tiger, to sleep again, unaware she was now an orphan.

***

The Wednesday after Columbus day, the air turning cool, Autumn tang in the air, Marty helped Dori secure her garden for the change of season, covering some plants up against the frost and bringing others inside. While they worked, Marty invited Dori to come over and see what she'd done to her apartment. "I found a beating heart under the floorboards last night."

"What?" Dori said, brushing a bit of dirt off her chin with the back of her thin liver-spotted hand.

"Well, I finally got around to taking the plastic off my futon, and when I moved it, I heard this thumping under the floorboards, and then I found this one loose floorboard, smaller than all the rest."

"The key slat," Dori provided.

"I guess, well, when I pulled it up, underneath the floor, between the slats or joists or whatever, was a battery-operated rubber heart, and it was sort of flopping and kicking. I guess a mouse or something ran over its ON switch. It scared me at first. You have to come by and see all the stuff I found in the closet. You won't believe it."

Dori walked back home with her that afternoon to check it out.

It was Marty's first guest she had invited back to her apartment and she felt self-conscious and a little nervous, but it was only Dori, so it would be fine.

She opened the door and called, "Five, we have company."

***

The tenant returned, but for the first time, she was not alone. The old woman who came in with her was a hag, a white-haired crone with one opaque gray eye and one tit. A good costume, except...she stunk of soil and fertilizer. The aroma emanated from her and the Apartment could taste its residue on Its walls. The same smell the tenant came in with whenever she was away for a long time. This hag was who she spent her time with when she wasn't home. This hag was the Apartment's rival.

***

"I've been here before," Dori said in awe. "This is Jerry-Jerome's place. And these...these are from his parties. I remember...this and that one."

The statement seemed to drain her of breath. Marty was expecting Dori to let out one of her

159

trademark cackles of delight, but instead the apartment silenced her.

"But," Dori said, more to herself than to Marty, "Jerry's been dead over 20 years, how...?"

Marty shrugged. "I found them in the closet. Well, most of it. I've added a few things myself. So you knew this guy?"

"I balled him," Dori said vacantly as her one good eye took all the Halloween decorations in. "I remember that wall of hands. Every Halloween party they'd goose me, like they were—Jerry never told me how he did it, how he made it work."

Marty wasn't sure what she meant. It weirded her out. Dori was always so sure about herself in every way, but now she looked doubtful.

Dori explored the rest of the apartment. She opened the wooden door of one of the kitchen cabinets suspended over the sink. Finally let out one of her standard cackles.

"You're Mother Hubbard! Your cupboard is bare."

Marty nodded, guiltily. "I've just been getting take-out since I moved in. Never been much of a cook. But I'm hoping—DORI!"

She'd been avoiding Dori's eyes as she spoke, instead gazing above her head and so saw that the top hinge of the tall kitchen cabinet was no longer connected. Its screws still hung in the hinge, but two inches separated it from the holes in the wall. Then the whole door came down like a butcher's cleaver!

Marty shoved Dori back, the flat of her hand over Dori's mastectomy scar, it saved her from getting brained, the edge of the door was aimed at her white-haired skull. But it still caught Dori a terrific blow on her right forearm and there was an audible SNAP of bone. Dori screamed briefly before her eyes rolled up in her head and she collapsed backward onto the floor in a heap.

Marty was surprised she didn't faint herself, instead she gained control. Her panic didn't matter, her shock didn't matter, all that mattered was helping Dori. She called for an ambulance, speaking in a clear, level voice like she was reporting the weather. Then she went back to Dori, checked she was breathing, she was but in a raspy wheeze.

Her right arm had acquired a second elbow four inches above her wrist, or so it seemed because it was bent there, giving the broken arm a zigzag pattern. Marty didn't dare touch it, but she straightened out Dori's legs, put a bunched-up t-shirt under her head and an overcoat over her. She sat down beside her on the floor and waited.

Dori's wrinkled eyelids fluttered and she opened her eyes.

"Marty?"

"Dori, don't move."

She licked her lips. "What happened?"

"The cabinet door fell off. It...the hinge came out. Dori...I think your arm is broken."

Dori blinked a few times, then tilted her chin and looked down at her right arm, lying in a zigzag pattern, and cackled. It was a weak laugh, but it was Dori.

"You *think* it's broken?! Honey, that *is* broken. Not the first time, but the first time there."

Marty tried to smile, but she could feel her upper lip crinkling and quivering.

"Marty, listen. I remembered something else about Jerry's apartment. I didn't want to tell you—"

"Shh, Dori, lie still. I called 911."

161

"After he died, an old woman who moved in here after hi—"

The downstairs buzzer buzzed. Marty got up and went to the intercom to buzz the EMS responders in, then went out to meet them.

When she got back, Dori was on the floor, trying to twist her body around, straining to get her left hand into the back right pocket of her cut-offs.

"Dori, lie still," Marty said, crouching beside her.

Dori stopped squirming.

"Well, then you get them!"

"What?"

"My keys, Marty. Take my keys."

"Okay."

She reached under Dori and fished out her ring of keys.

"Okay, I've got them, don't worry."

"Ma'm, we need to help your mother" one of the EMS guys gently pushed Marty away and started asking Dori questions as his partner began taking vitals and administering oxygen.

Before she answered them, Dori said to Marty, "Stay at my place."

"Don't worry, I'll keep an eye on your place."

"Don't stay here."

"Ma'm, you need to relax."

Dori lay back and let them get to work on her. They got her fastened to a gurney and carried out of the apartment and downstairs and to their van. Marty followed them without locking her door behind her.

"Is it okay if I come along with...my mother?" Marty asked, and she was allowed to ride with Dori to the Emergency Room of Bellevue Hospital.

She waited three hours or more, lost track of time just staring at the potted plants in the waiting room, in a fugue. A tall black nurse finally came out to speak with her and report that Dori was doing fine. Her broken arm had been set. She was now under sedation and the doctor wanted to keep her here for two days' observation.

"You might as well go home and get some rest, ma'm. Come back fresh tomorrow morning. And don't worry about your mother, she's got everybody in ward charmed already. She's pretty tough."

Marty nodded. "Thank you."

Marty left the hospital. Bellevue was on First Ave. and 31st. She walked the 23 blocks back to her apartment on St. Mark's Place.

***

It was the biggest mistake the Apartment ever made, but It didn't know that.

It had reacted as It saw fit. It hadn't planned to kill the old hag, but when the opportunity arose it was the most natural thing in the world to do. It had no regrets.

But in fact, both literally and figuratively, the Apartment had come unhinged.

***

When Marty got to her door, it was open a crack, how she had left when she followed Dori and the EMS guys out.

The lights were on.

She pushed the door open and walked in. The fallen cabinet door lay on the floor.

The tears came. And rage.

Marty screamed at the ceiling, "Why!" Her single shout reverberating against the walls.

163

She ran to her mattress and fell face down upon it and sobbed, the sobs wracking her chest like booted kicks. And running through her head a single prayer, "Let Dori be okay. Please God, let Dori be okay. Let Dori be okay. Let Dori be okay."

She felt responsible. If Dori hadn't become her friend, this wouldn't have happened to her. It was Marty's fault her friend was in the hospital.

"Let Dori be okay, let Dori be okay."

Eventually, she propped herself up on her elbows, wiped her face with her sleeves. She had to do more than pray to help her friend. She had to make a sacrifice.

She picked up the Hello Kitty bag and carried it to the bathroom. She unzipped it and upended it, emptying its contents, the remaining packets of White Tiger into the toilet.

WHAT ARE YOU DOING! STOP! the White Tiger roared in her head, in her body and her soul. DON'T!

Marty flushed. The packets swirled and collected at the center of the whirlpool.

Marty fought the urge to clutch at them—and won.

And then they were gone.

Except one, that bobbed up stubbornly and floated in the toilet.

Marty fished it out and dried it off against her shirt. She put it in the otherwise empty Hello Kitty bag and zipped it shut.

Just in case.

She left the bag on her mattress.

Then she grabbed her keys and Dori's keys and left the apartment.

For good.

***

The Apartment knew she would be back.

It wasn't worried.
She had to come back.
Halloween was coming.
She'd be back

***

After two days' observation, Dori was released with a cast on her arm. Marty helped her home. And stayed. Dori didn't ask and Marty didn't request it, but Marty would have fought like hell if Dori told her to go home. She knew the second she left, Dori would be out on the roof-garden, broken wing or not, tending to her garden. So instead Marty stayed and tended it to keep Dori from doing herself a mischief. Dori didn't object (for more reasons than one).

Marty learned how to cook, with Dori by her side, telling her what ingredients to put in and when and how, like the rat in Ratatouille. Marty felt like a real chef by the end.

On October 29th, while they ate a dinner of eggplant parmigiana they'd jointly constructed, Dori broached a subject that had been on her mind.

"I'd like to hire you."

"To do what?"

"What you're doing."

"You don't need to pay me, Dori."

"No. I know. But you need to get paid. It's only right. And, I have to confess, at my age...I need you, Marty. I want you to move in as my paid companion."

Marty took a sip of wine to hide the wrinkle of her upper lip.

"Okay," she said, into the wineglass.

That night they settled all the details. Dori had given it a lot of thought. She had even researched local movers to clear out Marty's apartment so she would never have to go back there. That was Dori for you, Marty thought, attention to every detail, though she sensed there was something else behind Dori's thoroughness.

And she was right. Being in the Apartment, Dori had sensed an otherness unlike anything she'd encountered in her long life and she rightly feared It, and it wasn't just about her appreciation of Marty— she'd have done the same for any random person she saw leaning too far off a subway platform, looking the wrong way as a train thundered in.

The only problem was, Dori was a handler. She'd handled things all her life, and she felt like she was handling adequately this threat to her friend, that she sensed more than believed in. Dori trusted her instincts more than her eyes and ears, and who can fault her in this instance?

But she didn't share her true thoughts and concerns with Marty, which led to the trouble.

Marty started calling her parents to let them know she was giving up the apartment, but she kept getting their answering machine. By October 30th, the machine was full.

So she sent them a postcard. "So long and thanks for all the fish," she wrote as a P.S., referencing Douglas Adams' *Hitchhiker's Guide to the Galaxy*.

She knew they'd never get .

She was right about that.

***

HALLOWEEN

***

No mistaking it. The day had a flavor unlike any other.

Crisp Autumn leaves.

Store-bought cobwebs—the Apartment proudly had the real thing—on trees and banisters. Pumpkins too early carved into Jack O Lanterns rotting on stoops up and down Saint Mark's Place.

On the morning of October 31st, about ten A.M., the teachers from a local pre-school on 9th Street and First Avenue, took their 3-6 year old students—banging drums and dressed in costumes of the Transformers, Princesses, Ninja Turtles, Batgirls, Ghosts, Witches, and WWE stars—on a parade around the neighborhood. Tenants from the other buildings across the street sat out on their stoops and applauded the children as they made their gala procession.

The Apartment relished it, wished It could have all those children inside It, dressed in their costumes. It would give them Halloween.

They were too far away, out of reach. But maybe one day...

But there was no mistaking the signs. Today was Halloween.

Tonight was the party.

She would come home.

The Apartment knew.

It wasn't worried.

Other people had come in, two days ago. Men in overalls. Their truck was still parked outside Its building (its windshield had already collected three parking tickets). Two men in overalls who tried to move out some of the furniture.

Not a problem. Like the flies, like the mice, like that man and that woman who tried to wake her, their dispatch was a mere reflex action for the Apartment.

All that mattered was that it was Halloween.

***

And, right or wrong, the monster was right.

Marty did return to the Apartment on Halloween.

It was 4 P.M. Dori was sprawled out on the couch taking a nap mid-Judge Judy. Marty didn't wake her, didn't need to, didn't need to leave a note. She was only popping out for a minute. She needed to get something.

She was only human.

She justified her actions, telling herself she was only going to pop in and grab what she needed. It was no big deal, so why not then? What was the big deal? But the fact of the matter was, like any other recurring addict, she needed her fix.

So she walked back to her apartment building on Saint Mark's Place.

First she checked her mail. Mostly sales fliers, but a letter from the landlords—Roethke and Roethke—requesting payment of October's rent. So her parents' had cut her off after all. Marty wasn't surprised.

She went upstairs, thinking about this, and entered #5.

She didn't lock the door behind her, just walked in and over to her futon to get what she came for.

It was a relief to have it back in her hands.

Clarissa, or The History of a Young Lady, by Samuel Richardson.

She had only a hundred-so pages to go. She needed to learn how Lovelace got his come-uppence, even though she loved him for all his villainy.

She clutched the brick of a book to her chest and turned...

Flop-kick.

Everything was different.

Flop-kick.

Or vastly more the same.

All around her was inky black. Tendrils of shredded black plastic garbage bags hung from the ceiling—where she had placed them, but they were thicker now, denser than she remembered—stretching out and around her, too vast and too close.

Flop-kick.

I am having some hallucinogenic episode, Marty told herself.

This was reasonable. She was a recovering drug addict and it was completely natural that symptoms of withdrawal might produce hallucinations.

You are okay. None of this is real.

But you need to find the door.

She took seven decisive steps forward and stopped. She took three more steps forward, but now with her hands out in front of her. Touching nothing, but torn shreds of plastic bags.

Her apartment wasn't that big. Was she was walking in circles? Was she walking at all? Was she dreaming all this?

She took another step with her hands outstretched and touched—

Another hand—and a cold finger entwined hers!

She jumped back. Focused.

The wall of hands in front of her.

Okay, okay, she told herself

That meant the windows were to her left and the door—the way out—to her right.

But Marty didn't move an inch. She stood her ground for several moments and considered.

***

Dori woke mid-way through Jeopardy, Halloween special edition, "Hotel where…"

"Marty…?" she called out.

***

Marty spoke to the Apartment.

"I'm leaving now."

***

The Apartment knew she was not leaving now. She was back. It was Halloween. Everything was as it should be. She wasn't leaving. She was never going to leave again. That was the problem, the Apartment had let her out before, but all this time during her absence—during her (forgiven) abandonment, the Apartment came to understand it was Its own fault. It hadn't adequately provided for her. But the Apartment was going to correct that, It had the power to correct that. It was Halloween after all and anything could happen.

***

For the fourth or fifth time, Marty set out to find the apartment door. She was convinced by now she was having a hallucination or a vivid dream, but it didn't seem to matter, the goal was to get out, regardless of the reality. All she needed to do was to find the doorknob. She'd abandoned *Clarissa*, somewhere along the line. To Hell with her.

Dismally, she thought, Shit, Dori will have woken up by now, I've got to…

She came to her front window, looking out on the sidewalk of Saint Mark's Place two stories down. The sun had set since she first came in. A clown in silk pajamas passed by beneath her accompanied by a Power Ranger. Next to the window was the giant white hand. Marty sat down in it, determined to ride things out.

She took deep breaths, oxygenating her system.

She tried to open the window.   It wouldn't budge.

Okay.   But it should be simple to get out now. A straight-line back from the window to the door.

She looked in the direction.   A football-field long repetition of hanging black streamers stretched before her telescopically.

Flop-kick.

***

At 7 P.M., Dori tuned in to NY1's telecast of the West Village's Halloween Costume parade.   She and Marty were going to watch it together.   Maybe she went to check it out in person, Dori thought, or, more accurately, hoped.

But Dori had never relied simply on hope.

She hunted around the living room until she found her Adidas sneakers and put them on.

***

Marty decided, it didn't matter how she got out of the apartment, as long as she got out, so instead of heading in the direction of the door, she moved from one window to the other, the one that opened onto the fire escape.   Here she had placed on the sill, the collection of a dozen life-like papier-mâché heads she found in one of the boxes from the closet.   She had formed them into a tiny pyramid.

But as she came to the window-well, the pyramid was no longer tiny, instead a barricade of heads stretched from the base of the window to the ceiling, papier-mâché heads, but so life-like and dead-like with patches of paper peeling off them, and all the mouths open, with a patchwork of paper teeth.

This is all a hallucination, Marty told herself against the evidence of her eyes. She waved her hand in front of her, trying to clear it like a wall of smoke. And quickly drew her hand back.

Ow. Her forefinger was bleeding. A papercut.

She looked up and all the heads were twitching, shifting, like a mound of Autumn leaves with something hiding under it.

She stepped away from it and collided with something that tinkled lightly like a windchime.

She reached out to steady herself and felt the circus-tent floor lamp. She leaned on it like a cane. Climbed it with her fingers until she found the dangling bead-chain and tugged it.

Darkness fled from the glare of the lamp. Marty stood in a cone of ordinariness cast by the light of the lamp. Just the ordinary floorboards around her. Nothing horrible. No hallucinations. But the light didn't stretch as far as the windows, instead just seemed to hug around her. She clung to the floor lamp's metal rod, to steady herself and not let go.

***

The Apartment always hated that lamp. To be honest, It hated all the furniture—the casket, the hand, the vanity—that the tenant had brought into It. Hate was too strong a word; the Apartment didn't "hate" anymore than It "loved," but it had an aversion to the furniture   They looked good—no denying that the tenant had good taste—but the Apartment could DO NOTHING with them. They weren't a part of the Apartment.

Things had started off bumpy this Halloween. Like all hosts, the Apartment was nervous, but It knew: it was early yet, parties always tended to go off later. It had to be patient, judge and trust to experience. The important thing was she was back on Halloween. It felt hollow that It had ever doubted she would return to It.

One way or another, she wasn't going to leave the Apartment again. It wasn't going to make that mistake again. No way.

What was lacking now was guests. Can't have a party without guests.

This year the Apartment had that covered.

It had guests on reserve for just such an occasion.

***

Out on the sidewalk Halloween was in bloom in the East Village that evening. Unlike other places, in the big city kids in their costumes didn't go door-to-door but store-to-store, stopping in at the bodegas, bars, restaurants, and newsstands to chant their plea of "Trick or treat!" Crisscrossing with them were adults in costumes, returning from the West Village parade. Draculas and Cuomos, Frankensteins and Dinkins, cheerleaders and giant dill pickles, a roll of Lifesavers with legs, a dachshund on a leash dressed up as a Chinese dragon.

Dori usually would have delighted in the sights, but she was scanning every passerby for Marty, even as she dreaded where she knew she would find her.

I should have said something to her, Dori scolded herself. But what was there to tell, a lot of little stories she'd been told over the years? There are a thousand such stories in the big city and they usually are just that, stories.

Usually.

Dori quickened her pace to Saint Mark's Place.

***

Marty tried to drag the lamp with her to light her way. It slid easily along the floor but the cord was short and only got her to the center of the apartment and her futon.

Flop-kick.

The Hello Kitty bag was on the futon. Her last packet of White Tiger was inside it.

Flop-kick.

Maybe that's what she needed, maybe that's what would make this all go away.

Flop-kick.

Hair of the dog. Whisker of the White Tiger.

She sank down on her knees.

Marty unzipped the bag.

It was empty!

Flop-kick.

Wait, uh, no. it was there, stuck to the inside of the bag.

Flop-kick.

She ripped it out and ripped it open and poured the White Tiger on the web between her forefinger and thumb, and lowered her head to inhale –

But just then the "guests" arrived.

***

They made a peremptory noise as they presented themselves for the gala. Like a fussy person opening up their morning newspaper and shaking out the pages. Only, this sound was all around, surrounding her, a chorus of fussy newspaper shakers, closing in on her from every corner of the room.

The ten missing co-workers of Gerard Baldyga oozed from the walls of the Apartment. They'd each seen better days, but their long entombment and mummification in the Apartment's walls had aged them to perfection, like dried flowers pressed in a book .

They presented themselves in their tatters. A naked ivory pelvis bone exposed through a rotting pairs of Chinos. A gaudy agate necklace rattling against xylophone ribs. Empty black eye sockets behind Gucci designer frames.

They emerged and hung fastened in place by their vertebrae in the studs of the Apartment's walls.

***

The White Tiger on Marty's hand scattered like pixie dust as she shrank away from the nearest desiccated corpse, grabbing onto the floor lamp like a lifeline.

And in doing so, pulling it too far away from the wall socket.

Unplugging it.

Plunging herself into nightmarish black again.

But worse.

She no longer believed this was hallucination. She was starting to believe it was a judgment on her. She'd been half trying to kill herself with drugs and bad decisions for the last few years, so she felt she deserved whatever was happening to her, and she wasn't going to fight back.

But then Dori showed up.

***

Dori looked up from the sidewalk to Marty's apartment windows. They were dark, reflecting the streetlights and the bare limbs of the elm tree.

At the entryway door, Dori pushed all the buttons for all the apartments, not caring which one of them buzzed her in. It was Halloween, so five or six chimed in and kept ringing, and she heard a few voices call down from two floors up, "This way."

When Dori got to the first landing and looked down the hall, the door of #5 swung open.

***

Finally, a guest.   Welcome.

***

Marty sprang off the futon in the direction of the door buzzer.   She should be able to find the door, even with her eyes closed.   She crawled on her hands and knees.   Her left hand landed on something that felt like a step.

It was *Clarissa*.

Then light flooded into the apartment from the hallway as the door swung open.   Stale, clear, sane fluorescent light.   And silhouetted in the doorway, a frazzled-hair figure in a dark windbreaker, with only one arm in a sleeve.

"Dori!"

Marty got to her feet, still clutching *Clarissa*, and ran to her.

And Dori came in too far.

"No!" Marty shouted, but the door slammed shut.

She ran forward and—Clonk!   She and Dori knocked heads.   But even as they momentarily saw stars in front of their eyes, they didn't separate, holding onto each other, each with their one free arm.

Dori said, "Marty, gotta get the hell outta here."

Outta here, outta here.

Dori's voice echoed like they were in an airplane hangar or an underground cavern.

"Been trying," Marty said.

Trying, trying.

"Hold onto me."

Me, me.

"Not letting go."

Go, go.

Dori spoke in a whisper, "Which way to the door? I can't see a thing."

"Me neither," Marty whispered back.

Gradually though, she made out a trace of light on the floor, streetlight coming in through the window that overlooked the sidewalk.   Filtered through the bare branches of the elm tree outside, the orange-light cast skittering tarantula shadows across the floor.

"This way," Marty said.   It was in the wrong direction, but it was a connection with the outside world, the "real world" as she thought of it now.

As they inched their way toward the light, the guests sticking out of the walls rattled their dry bones at them like bamboo windchimes.

"Ignore them," Marty said, to herself as much as Dori.   "Don't mingle."

Dori cackled nervously.

Marty's left shoulder bumped into something.   It was her floorlamp again.   Top-heavy with its stained-glass circus-tent shade, it tottered dangerously but stayed upright.

"Dori, stay here."

"What...?"

"I'm going to plug in the lamp."

She left Dori standing in the scant light from the window.   She got down on her hands and knees, and followed the electrical cord back to its plug.   The lamp had helped before.   She found the plug and, dimly, the wall socket, but the plug didn't reach. Duh.   She had to move the floorlamp closer, but she couldn't just yank the cord because—

Dori yelped and there was a thud that Marty felt in her hands and knees.

She swung round.   But everything seemed to be all right (relatively) at first.   Dori was still standing where she left her, only now...she looked shorter. She realized that she couldn't see Dori's white Addidas sneakers, just her bare ankles.

The floorboards Dori was standing on had dropped below the level of the floor, so now she stood sunk in the well between the lower slats. She didn't dare move right or left, forward or backward, just held her balance and looked curiously down at what had happened. She wasn't hurt. She stood in the same place only six inches lower, perched on one end of the floorboards, while the other end stood high, angled on a fulcrum of the cross-joist, like a see-saw.

Flop-kick!

It happened too fast and Marty was too far away to prevent it, to stop it from happening, to save her friend Dori.

***

The Apartment welcomed the arrival of the Hag. It knew she would come to the party. It knew she was the reason the new tenant had abandoned It. It was happy to have her back inside of It. It wanted another crack at her and this time It wouldn't miss.

So It opened Its door. It allowed their reunion. It even gave them light to draw them closer to Its window. All that was necessary was the correct positioning. Patience.

The Apartment had a favorite ill-illusion that It still needed to enact. A Halloween tradition. The bloody broken window. The Hag just had to stand in just the right place.

***

Perversely, Marty thought of her favorite movie, *Beetlejuice*, a scene at the end where two of the vacuous party guests are laughing at the after-dinner supernatural display unbeknownst to them that a carnival "Test-Your-Strength" contraption is being erected behind them, and that when Bettlejuice's mallet-shaped hands come down they shoot straight up through the ceiling.

So quick, there wasn't time for Marty to scream.

The high end of the floorboards pivoted down in one swift incredible motion. And at the other end, Dori was catapulted into the air. She arced backwards and sailed straight for the window pane behind her. A homerun ball.

Like most catastrophes, Marty witnessed it in a kind of slow motion, impotent to stop it, damned to watch it play out. Dori's light thin frame hurtling towards the glass.

A flash of white.

And then it became not just slow-motion, but no motion. Dori suspended in air. A freeze-frame.

But not suspended in air, but seated—cupped—in the giant white hand chair, that had shot up from the floor—its truncated wrist becoming a muscular forearm—and caught her, like an outfielder snagging a bases-loaded flyball before it went over the homerun fence, ending the game.

The hand slowly lowered, its base becoming once more a wrist.

Dori descended like she was in a pneumatic barbershop chair, until her Addidas were back on the ground.

Dori let out a nervous, involuntary cackle. "Woo-wee!"

Marty didn't stop to wonder. She yanked on the floorlamp's cord, getting the extra inch, and inserted its plug into the wall socket. The lamp tottered but stood its ground and lit up the room around her. Everything looked normal.

"We're leaving," Marty said, but she wasn't speaking to Dori.

She stood up and walked over to Dori, helped her to her feet. Leaning against each other, they started in the direction of the apartment's door, then Marty stopped. She went over to the giant white hand and, grabbing it by its thumb, carried it back with her to Dori.

Guided by the light of the floorlamp, they traveled across the apartment's scant expanse until they came to the door.

Marty grabbed the doorknob and turned. Her sweaty hand just slid around the knob, it wouldn't turn. She wanted to cry, instead—as crazy as it felt—she stepped back, lifted the white hand up in front of her, aiming it like a bazooka, and she touched the tip of the forefinger to the doorknob.

And the door opened.

She shoved Dori out into the hallway, followed by the hand, and was just about to leave herself when— *Clarissa.*

She turned around. The book was on the floor in the middle of the room, well in the reach and protection of the floorlamp's glare.

Marty went back for it, reached down and grabbed it.

The apartment door slammed shut.

And then Marty's parents came out to surprise her.

Her father oozed out of the bathroom. The shape of her father, his likeness, but he was greenish and glistened like an expectorated glob of phlegm as he shuffled toward her, leaving behind him a snail's trail of lougy.

Her mother came out of the closet. She was white as plaster. She was plaster, just a cast of her mother. But she moved, reaching out both her arms, both her beautifully clawed hands for Marty.

Marty backed away, deeper into the apartment, whimpering, "Mummy, Daddy," like she was three years old again.

She could hear Dori hammering on the door with her one good fist.

But louder than that pounding was another noise, growing in volume.

Flop-kick, FLOP-kick, FLOP-KICK!

She looked to the hole in the floor where the rubber battery-operated heart was nested. It seemed to be glowing now with its own reddish incandescence . Marty stared down at it, fascinated despite her fear, and she made a decision.

Turning her back on the advance of her dead parents, Marty lifted her hardcover copy of *Clarissa* over her shoulder and chucked it at the window with all her might. It hit dead center and shattered the glass with a brittle crash. Even before the shower of shards struck the pavement below, Marty was crouched at the hole in the floor, reaching in, her fingers primed like talons. She fastened on the beating heart and dug in. It writhed and fought against her grip. She yanked but the heart held tight like an embedded tick. She squatted and braced herself and then pulled at it with both hands and lifting with her knees. It came free with a lurch that landed her on her ass. Marty held the beating heart aloft before her, like a midwife displaying a newly delivered baby, and the heart fought and squirmed in the same irritable agitated fashion of a new-born.

Marty twisted around and threw it overhand out the window's jagged hole.

Everything stopped, everything but Dori's incessant battering on the apartment door.

Marty closed her eyes. She stood up and blindly staggered in the direction of the sound, not stopping until she was flat against the door and could feel Dori's frantic knocks from the other side.

She fumbled for the doorknob, found it, and turned it.

The door opened and Dori almost fell in. Instead she yanked Marty out, by the shoulder and pulled her to her. Marty opened her eyes, blinking against the brightness of the hallway fluorescent lights.

"I'm okay," she said, in answer to the fierce hug Dori was giving her.

Dori relaxed her grip.

They walked like two drunks down the stairwell, holding onto each other, AND onto the giant white hand chair, which made getting down the stairs a bit tricky, but they weren't about to abandon it just yet.

A small group of on-lookers were gathered outside the building as they descended the front stoop. They were all looking up at the broken window, and not paying any attention to the old lady with her arm in a cast and the young lady carrying a giant white hand. Police sirens howled in the distance, but being New York City on Halloween, they might've been headed a dozen other places. A broken window hardly merited a 911 call.

Once on the sidewalk, Marty walked over to where the glass from the window had landed in a mass of chips and shards. And the rubber heart was on top of it, still beating, but feebly, a wheezy whir to its internal mechanisms. Marty stepped around it, searching until she found *Clarissa*. She picked up the book. Damn you, Samuel Richardson, the ending better be good.

The on-lookers dispersed—nothing more happening, show over—they had parties to get to, hook-ups to hook to; the night wasn't over, there would be plenty more broken windows to gape at.

Dori was seated in the white hand, like a queen on her throne, but she stood up as soon as Marty came back.

Marty said, "Let's go home."

Dori cackled in agreement.

Wordlessly, they left the hand behind on the sidewalk.

***

The party was over.

The Apartment felt dejected.

Not about the loss of the heart.   The heart It could live without, after all it had only been a decoration, a rubber battery-operated prop.   The original had been made of Jell-O and a nylon stocking.   If the Apartment wanted to It could fashion another, or else, salvage one from the offal.

But It was disappointed in the new tenant.

She hadn't looked back, not once, back up at Its window as she walked away.

It was as if the Apartment no longer existed for her.

She wouldn't be back.   The Apartment knew.

Maybe this would be Its last Halloween party.   It didn't know.

Better to sleep.

***

"Hey, guys, check this out!"

"What?'

"What?"

"What"

"I think it's a party."

The apartment door was ajar.

A collection of people were out in the hallway, gabbling.

A knock on the door.

"Hello?"

The door opened.

"Oh, my God, guys, you got to see this!"

"Whoa!"

"Whoa!"

"Whoa..."

"This guy decorated his place like a Haunted House."

"Hello...?"

"Maybe he went out to get something."

"Or maybe it's part of the Haunted House. Ha ha, we come in and he jumps out in a hockey mask with a chainsaw or something."

"Let's check it out."

The door opened wide and they all came inside It.

Five people, three men, two women, all dressed as Bicycle-back playing cards. The men were the King of Clubs, the Jack of Diamonds, and the Ace of Spades. The women were the Queen of Hearts and a Joker, and they went ooo and ahh and the Queen fake-screamed.

***

Party-crashers.

Well, it was still Halloween. Why waste the night?

The Apartment let them come in and be part of the party, even though Its heart wasn't really in It anymore.

But It could always salvage one from the offal.

***

It was the disappearance of the two furniture movers who left their truck parked across the street from the building, but otherwise evaporated from the map, which led to the landlords (now called Roethke

Brothers) to take Apartment #5 off the market again. Indefinitely.   Their father—may he rest in peace—had been right, the unit was a jinx.   It was cheaper, less of a headache and a hassle not to rent it.   They could take the hit.   In fact, they were considering renovating—gutting—the whole building in a few years and rewiring and rebuilding all the units as condominiums.   So renting or not renting unit #5 was not an issue.   They could afford to wait, more than they could afford another incident.

***

The Apartment knew It could wait, too.

There was always another Halloween.

THE END?

APARTMENT 5 IS ALIVE

Special signed and numbered editions of this book accompanied by a signed and numbered print by artist Linda Wulkun are available. This edition is:

#_____ of _____ copies

Made in the USA
Middletown, DE
23 February 2021